Clipped!

By Patricia Curren

INFINITY
PUBLISHING

ISBN 978-1-4958-0076-4
ISBN 978-1-4958-0077-1 eBook

Printed in the United States of America

Published September 2014

INFINITY PUBLISHING
1094 New DeHaven Street, Suite 100
West Conshohocken, PA 19428-2713
Toll-free (877) BUY BOOK
Local Phone (610) 941-9999
Fax (610) 941-9959
Info@buybooksontheweb.com
www.buybooksontheweb.com

Acknowledgements

Like any first novel, *Clipped!* has experienced numerous changes. It needed the touch of many helping hands along the way.

A huge thank you goes out to the phenomenal women of my critique group, The Scribe Tribe, who persevered through the final draft of the book.

Special appreciation goes to Michele Sheppard, Children's Librarian for the Red Mountain branch of the Mesa Public Library, Teresa Becker, Copy Editor, Rachel Cupryk, head of the English Department at Red Mountain High School, and especially to Kendell, my teen beta reader.

This story wouldn't have survived even a first draft without the encouragement of my family: Jean, Beverly, Vicki, Robin, Victoria, Melodie, Dorothy and Raye. The years flowed by and two of you are no longer with us, but I feel you watching and know you are happy for me.

Finally, I'll always be grateful to Tom Spille, who gave his honest opinion throughout the entire process. Not a writer, he's the consummate artist and has an ear for what rings true. I only wish I could critique his outstanding paintings with the same skill.

Chapter 1

Unaware that her feet barely touched the floor or how tightly she gripped her calligraphy pen, Kendra Morgan labored over her paper, intent on each stroke. Concentrating even harder than usual, she tried to forget the ache she felt at the loss of her friend, Cloud Nicholson. Today a snippet of conversation she'd overheard between two men at the corner store kept repeating in her head.

"The paper didn't say much, but Harold Upstead claims he heard on his police scanner that the detectives had never seen such an unsettling crime scene," the first man said as he scanned his groceries.

"Yeah, basically all I've read in the Morning Sun or seen on television was that she'd been viciously attacked and murdered. I wonder if she suffered a lot before she died?" the other man drawled as if he were discussing something as common as the day's weather forecast.

"Boy, you're a gruesome one! I don't even want to know stuff like that! Let me know if Harold hears anything else though, will ya? I sure hope the cops get some leads. It's a damned shame, that poor girl." The man grabbed his groceries and hurried out the door.

Wherever Kendra went — the store, the school, the library — it didn't matter — the talk centered on Cloud's disappearance. She had vanished while on the way home from her cousin's birthday party. A few days later, her brutalized body had been discovered. Now Kendra sighed and pushed the memory of the conversation from her mind. Instead, she focused on the last few minutes of her calligraphy project at the community center.

The curve of the letters would please anyone, but the feel of the pen in her hand as it glided over the page was what transported Kendra. A little smile crept across her face and into the dark corners of hurt in her heart. For a short time Kendra was transported to a place that was good, a place that was safe.

At the beginning of summer, when she'd first moved to Finchville, Nebraska, her mom had urged her to take a class at the community center as a way to meet some kids her age.

"If you don't make some friends soon, it's going to be a boring summer for you. As long as it's free I think you should give it a try, Kendra. If you don't like it you can always quit. I won't be out any money, and you've got lots of time," her mom said.

Now that Kendra had made some friends at school and Audrey Worth had become her very-best-friend-in-all-the-world, she didn't need the calligraphy class. But she'd signed up for the advanced class in the fall anyway. Every Saturday afternoon she found her spine curved into the molded chair. She leaned over her work to marvel at the artful permanence of the letters flowing from the tip of her pen.

I can make each one exactly as Mrs. Oakley showed us the first week of class, she mumbled to herself. *I can make the "s" perfectly. My "z" looks awesome. I can even control the "w."* That was more than Kendra could say about the rest of her life.

"All right everyone, it's two o'clock. That's it for today." Mrs. Oakley's voice interrupted Kendra's bliss. Reluctantly she carried her materials to the front of the class, grabbed her jacket and stopped at the water fountain in the hall.

As she bent to drink, a spot of color in the next classroom caught her eye. She stepped closer to be sure she was seeing what she thought she was seeing. It was Cloud's hair clip — the one with the crystals that shone so brightly! It was sticking out of a man's pocket! Since Cloud's aunt had brought it as a gift from Sweden, Cloud had worn it nearly every day to school. Kendra told herself to breathe, but it seemed like too much to do.

Besides Audrey, Kendra had liked Cloud the best of all of her other classmates even though Cloud had a reputation for being a bit of a bad girl. She seemed to lead with her desires instead of common sense. That often took her down a trail of trouble.

The night before classes began at Spencer Middle School, Cloud had hacked into the school's computer system and changed all the student room assignments for 1st period. The chaos that followed earned her a seven-day suspension, which her wealthy parents protested so vigorously that it was reduced to one day.

Audrey said she liked Cloud because she was so funny — always cracking jokes, sometimes not very kind — but so darned daring that she'd have to laugh anyway. But Kendra admired Cloud for doing whatever she wanted, and damn the consequences. Now Cloud was gone and all Kendra had were a few memories of her friend. And the knowledge that even fourteen-year-olds die.

Kendra shuddered at this gruesome thought, then drew a ragged breath and gathered the courage to look once again at the barrette peeping from the man's jeans pocket. She recognized him as that weird guy Mom called developmentally disabled. She'd seen him around town at different times, usually delivering newspapers. Now he loomed over a teenage boy as they sat at a table assembling a model of some kind. He was oblivious to Kendra's stare as he concentrated on the small plastic pieces before him.

Kendra wondered how something that belonged to Cloud could've found its way into his pocket. *Surely he couldn't be the killer? And why am I the one who spotted it? I've got enough problems already. We're getting settled again, away from the trouble Dad brings to our lives. I have a new school and kids I like.* She stumbled down the hall and out of the building. *What if he just found the clip somewhere and I tell on him and he's not bright enough to defend himself? I'd feel terrible.*

Mechanically, Kendra walked toward home. Becoming aware of the maple and oak leaves rustling beneath her shoes, she began to relax a bit. She wanted to forget the whole thing, but knew she couldn't. Wishing with all her might that she hadn't been the one to see and recognize her friend's barrette, there it was — staring her in the face. *No use trying to avoid it. I have to do the right thing,* she thought. Her steps quickened.

Rounding the corner at Marsh and State Streets, she could see Mr. Thomas' house and his preschool son in pursuit of a cat. She stuffed down her feeling of jealousy at the sight of the little guy playing happily behind the white picket fence. *Must be nice to have a nice house and parents who dote on you,* she thought.

Mr. Thomas was her homeroom teacher and she had decided he was okay, as far as teachers went. At the start of the school year he told the class if they had anything — anything at all — to talk about, he was always available. He had even invited the class to his home for a barbecue at the start of the school year. Surely Mr. Thomas would listen to her. More importantly, she could hand this problem off to him.

"Why Kendra Morgan, what brings you by today?" His tone seemed pleasant enough, but looking past him she saw several grown-ups in the living room and smelled chicken frying. A banner of blue letters on a silver background spelled out "HAPPY BIRTHDAY!"

You dummy, Kendra. What are you thinking, coming to a teacher's home? And interrupting a party besides, she thought.

He held the door open for her to enter the empty hallway.

"I've got something important to tell you, Mr. Thomas. Maybe I should come back another time?"

"No, no, Kendra, it's fine. Not to worry. What's on your mind?" He shifted his feet back and forth.

"It's about Cloud Nicholson," she stammered. "I saw something at the community center that should be reported to the police. I knew you'd know what to do."

"Oh really?" He stopped sidestepping and looked hard at Kendra.

"Yes, I saw a guy; I think his name is Billy Ray. I heard a lady call him that one day when he was delivering papers. Anyway, when I saw him today he had Cloud's hair clip in his pocket! Do you think he might have had something to do with her murder?"

Mr. Thomas' eyebrows went up. "How do you know it was hers?"

"I know. It was her favorite, a one-of-a-kind." Kendra shot back.

"Kendra, from a distance it may've looked like Cloud's barrette, but you could be wrong. Or if it was hers, he could've found it somewhere. Accusing someone of such a serious thing can ruin people's lives." He gestured her toward the door. "If you want, we can talk about it more on Monday morning."

"Yes, Mr. Thomas," she muttered, stumbling on the last two porch steps. Anger rose from the pit of her stomach. *It's like he doesn't even believe me!* she thought. *Why did he put me off? Just because I played a prank or two?*

She recalled how she'd snuck into his classroom and replaced his CD of Lincoln's Gettysburg address, which the class was memorizing, with a Taylor Swift CD. His look of astonishment when Swift's voice replaced "Four score and seven years ago..." was priceless. The roar of laughter from the class had been well worth the punishment that followed.

Cloud was really the one who had planned the joke. Even though Kendra knew that replacing the CD might get her in hot water, she had decided it was worth the risk to be accepted into Cloud's posse.

Kendra knew how to fit in. That was one of the things she'd learned from the many moves they'd made, trying to stay one step ahead of Dad. Staying mum for the entire two weeks of cleaning the whiteboards was hard, but no way would she be a rat.

Now she pushed herself to get home; being late meant trouble, especially if Mom had supper ready. Tired and hungry, a spot behind her right eye began to throb, sending blinding flashes of light that blocked the autumn sun's rays. She wanted to think of another plan, but the pain and the fresh memory of Mr. Thomas' disbelief made it impossible. So hoping Mom wouldn't be too angry, she pulled her coat to her thin frame as a cold wind lifted her fine blonde hair with its harsh fingers.

*****

"Kendra Kay, where have you been?"

"Sorry Mom..."

"Your sister and I have already finished. I was worried about you, with that killer on the loose." Teresa Morgan scratched at an angry red rash on her inner arm. "Well, what's left is on the stove. Help yourself."

"Okay, Mom," Kendra replied. No use trying to tell her about what she'd seen, at least not right now. The pain behind her eye now circled her head. She knew she had to eat and lie down in a dark place, fast. Sleep was the only thing that helped her migraines.

Mom couldn't afford to take her to the doctor unless she was really sick, but she'd read about migraines at school. According to a website on Google, allergies, fatigue and stress were some of the things that triggered them. Kendra didn't think she had allergies and she slept plenty. That left stress. Well, that shouldn't be a big surprise. Mom's stress showed up as that red, itchy rash on her arms. It seemed to Kendra that Mom was always applying Aveeno Skin Relief cream. Yes, stress had hung its shingle at the Morgan household for a very long time.

She grabbed a bent fork and carried her plate to the table while her mother went to answer the phone. Good — no more lecture right now. The pot roast had a layer of gel coating it, and the boiled potatoes were grayish and half warm. She managed to eat a little by pouring ketchup over everything, and washing it down with milk. Then she left her plate in the rust-stained sink and crept into bed.

Chapter 2

Powdered sugar donuts and coffee were Kendra's favorite and usual breakfast on school mornings. The way the powdered sugar melted when it touched her tongue caused her mouth to water; then a gulp of strong, black coffee would cut the sweetness so she could take another bite. Other kids' moms cooked oatmeal and stuff for breakfast, but that wasn't the way the Morgans did it.

Mom was long gone to her job when the kitchen clock showed it was time to deliver Kendra's sister, Toni, to Little Rabbit Day Care.

"It's time to go," Kendra grabbed her coat and headed to the living room. Four-year-old Toni sat rocking back and forth against the hard back of the sofa, grasping one curl between her first and second finger and stroking it with her thumb, her legs straight out in front of her. A veil lifted from her blue eyes as she turned from the morning cartoons at Kendra's prompting.

"You're not ready!" Kendra cried. "Where are your shoes? You're going to make me late and I've got to talk to Audrey before school!"

Toni's feet barely hit the floor as Kendra towed her toward the bedroom. "Now find your shoes, quick!" she demanded, frantically scanning the cluttered floor.

"Here they are, Kendra." Toni's voice squeaked as she pulled the missing shoes from her toy box.

"Okay, sit down. I'll put them on for you just this one time!" *How could she look so sweet, yet be so much trouble?* Kendra thought. *It makes me so mad that I have to take care of Toni when it's really Mom's job*! Then a hot wave of guilt flooded through her. *Of course, Mom's just doing her best to keep our family going*. How could she even think of being angry with her? *And Toni's just being a little kid.*

Arriving at the day care, she gave her sister a big hug. "I didn't mean to yell at you earlier, Toni. You know I love you, right?" She hung Toni's coat on a little peg.

"Lub you, too."

"Okay, you have a good day, little Munchketeer." She gently tousled her soft ringlets.

Toni laughed at Kendra's nickname for her, hugged Kendra's waist and ran to greet her playmates.

*****

Kendra met Audrey at their usual spot by the Circle K. As they walked to school she told Audrey what she'd seen at the community center that had turned her already jumbled world completely on its head.

"You've got to be kidding!" Audrey's eyes widened.

"I wish I were," Kendra continued. "I got the bright idea to tell Mr. Thomas, but he didn't even believe me! All I got for my trouble was a lecture."

"I guess you shouldn't have played that prank in class. He probably thought you were up to more trouble. I sure thought it was cool though," Audrey's voice trailed off.

"Yeah, I 'spose you did since you weren't the one cleaning whiteboards forever."

"Geez, Kendra, I can't believe you were brave enough to go to Mr. Thomas on your own. This whole thing blows me away. Totally."

"Does that mean you won't go to the cops with me?"

"You've got to be kidding, Kendra! No way!"

"All you have to do is tag along. I just need you there, so I'm not alone. I can't do it by myself," Kendra pleaded.

"Why don't you ask your mom to go with you?"

"She only takes time off work if it's a national emergency."

"I think you've got one."

Kendra shook her head hard.

"At least tell her," Audrey countered.

*****

It was late afternoon and Kendra wasn't sure how long she'd been standing there, a safe distance from the police station. Her feet felt glued to the sidewalk, unable to go forward or back. Throughout the day she had tried to imagine the best way to tell her story, but nothing seemed right.

Her only real experience with police had been less than a year earlier when Dad had bullied his way into their apartment. He was drunk and looking for more liquor to quench his unquenchable thirst. Kendra remembered the soft sound the flour-coated pork chop made as it fell from Mom's hand when he grabbed her. The gentle plopping noise seemed odd in the midst of the loud words and the awful look Mom got when he hit her.

As she bent over in pain, she told him where she'd hidden the vodka. When he turned away, Kendra rushed to her side to hear Mom whisper, "Run downstairs and call the cops."

In spite of the fear coursing through her veins as she raced down the stairs, she felt a thrill knowing she was doing something to help Mom. But when the landlady opened the door and Kendra blurted out why she needed to use the phone, the thrill was replaced with embarrassment. She recognized that look of scorn.

The woman allowed her to use the phone, but her body language made it clear — she wasn't happy to help.

Kendra didn't know how much more of Dad's behavior she could stand. He continued to follow them from town to town, causing humiliating scenes. Before long, the neighbors were looking down their noses at Kendra and her family like they were poor, white trash.

Worse yet, she couldn't stand seeing Mom being used as a punching bag. When the officers arrived, they asked Kendra's mom if she was all right, and took her report. As they hauled Dad out the door, they said they could put him in jail, but not for long. Kendra slumped onto the sofa feeling hopeless. What good were the police if they couldn't even stop a drunk from hurting his family?

Suddenly Kendra found herself backing away from the police station. Wheeling around, she headed home hating herself for her cowardice.

Then a face, a face and a uniform popped into her mind: it was Brent Grimsby who worked at the bus depot where Mom worked. He had been hired to stop a flurry of break-ins at the lockers several months ago. Even after the break-ins stopped, he had stayed on, patrolling inside and out with his long rambling stride, Maglite swinging like a pendulum at his side.

Brent was always friendly to Toni and her when they went into the bus depot's café where Mom worked. He'd call, "Hi there, dolls. Where'd you get those blonde curls? Did you know they bounce like Slinkys when you walk?"

They would giggle and duck their heads. If she hurried, maybe she could catch him going on his lunch break. He worked a later shift so it made sense to her that his lunch would be about four o'clock.

Flying around the corner, she headed for the employees' entrance. Boomph. Her nose met something flat and hard. "Ouch! Sorry Brent, I was hoping to catch you." Kendra rubbed her nose, eyeing his massive chest.

"Well you caught me all right. Wish more girls wanted to do that." He stooped to retrieve his cigarette from the sidewalk. "What's your rush?"

"I… I need your help. It's important."

"Why you can have anything you want, sweetheart, anything at all." His eyes narrowed as his lips pulled on the cigarette. He ran his long fingers through his greasy, dark hair. "C'mon, tell 'ol Brent all about it." He put his hand on her opposite shoulder so she had to walk close to him. Kendra didn't like his touch so she pulled away and rushed headlong into her story. While she talked, she noticed he glanced sideways at her, saying nothing except an occasional "Hmm."

When she finished, Brent stopped and looked up and down the street.

Kendra turned to face him.

"That's quite a story, Kendra, but you know what? I believe you. You know what else?" He watched her closely as he spoke. "No one else will. Not unless I convince them somehow. Sure. I'm not a real cop, but I am paid to make certain no one breaks the law where I work. That counts for something. All the same, it's going to be a tough job to persuade the police. So I should get something for my trouble, don't you think?"

Kendra started to ask what and stopped. Brent was staring at her, his dark eyes intent, knowing. In one nanosecond, Kendra recognized his hungry gaze, even though no man had ever looked at her that way before. He reached out as if to touch her cheek, but she drew back.

Shrugging his shoulders, he said, "Come on Kendra, you're filthy cute and you know it." Then he turned and sauntered away.

For a moment Kendra wanted to cry at the thought of what Brent had suggested with just a look and a few flirtatious words. Instead she turned toward home. Terror and shame ran with her down the darkening street. She gasped for breath and her side hurt, but her legs wouldn't stop running. The streets didn't look the same anymore, nor did the houses. Their windows were like eyes — peering into the depths of her very soul.

Chapter 3

Julie, the receptionist at the law firm of Tuttle and Bernhardt, had left the switchboard to make copies for a client when the phone lines began flashing. Peg Strong, the office manager, put line one on hold and was helping the person on two when a third line started ringing and blinking. "Cliff, will you catch line three?" she yelled to the legal assistant as she scratched her head in frustration. After several more rings, he finally picked it up. Peg had hired him three months ago and she knew his slow response wasn't because he was too busy. He just didn't believe he should be required to answer the phones. It was beneath him. *I really need to get out of here today,* she thought, *but first I've got to get this cleared up.* Peg stomped from her cubicle to his and stood with hands on hips, waiting for him to look up from his work.

"Sorry I took so long getting that call. You'd think Julie could at least cover the switchboard, wouldn't you?" Cliff whispered as he looked up.

"Oh, are you afraid she'll hear your catty remark?" Peg hissed and motioned towards Julie's desk. "I'd like to see you do her job for just one day! I know you think your position is much more important and demanding than hers, but it's not!

She contributes as much to the success of this office as you do." Peg's face felt red hot. "I expect you to be a part of the team here and that means jumping on the phones by the third ring."

"Sorry, Peg. I'll do better going forward." The stunned look on Cliff's face told her that her words had an impact. Immediately she felt her heart rate returning to normal. She gave him a curt nod, grabbed her jacket and sandwich and bolted for the building entrance for her usual sanity-saving lunchtime walk.

Julie smiled and gave Peg the okay sign as she hurried toward the door. Julie's reaction showed that she had heard the tirade, and appreciated Peg's support.

Peg took a deep breath and started along the boulevard, recalling a riddle she'd heard earlier about men's shortcomings. "What is the difference between men and government bonds? — The bonds mature."

So this fine fall day, Peg entered Carlisle Park with a smile on her face. She took in the sights and sounds, always on the lookout for something unusual, like the territorial crow which sometimes dive-bombed her as she traveled through his turf.

Today — October 21st — didn't disappoint. As she headed off the trail toward a picnic table, something caught her eye. A box of animal cookies, a package of cheese curls, a loaf of white bread, and a bag of mini-bagels were neatly lined up in the grass. They were all opened, as if ready for diners. Someone had taken great care to arrange them. Peg marveled at who might have left this odd display and why.

She heard a sound and glanced back to see a big man watching her from a nearby stand of cottonwood trees. Realizing she was alone in an isolated spot, Peg turned quickly towards the trail.

"Wait, where you going?"

Peg paused and scrutinized him. His head was large and round and sat too far forward on his body. His eyes and face were round. No corners, no angles — just round.

He rubbed his stubbly beard and stared back.

"I've got to get back to work," she said quickly.

"I saw you looking at my presents. What do you think? Will my critters like what I did?" He paused a moment as though searching for words. "I worked hard getting them ready. Mama says it's good to have things neat. Do you think they look neat?"

"Sure, they look great, but I've got to get back now." She kicked at the dirt with the toe of her shoe. The thought of all that power paired with diminished mental capacity scared the heck out of her. *Way too unpredictable,* she thought.

"You do? You really like them?" Eagerly he rubbed his palms on his pants legs. "Thanks, lady."

Peg hurried away before he could say anything else. *Whew, what was that all about?* she mused as she recovered her composure.

*****

Billy Ray settled himself on the ground against one of the cottonwoods. The bark of the tree scratched his back where his shirt had escaped the elastic of his underwear. Unaware of the October dampness soaking into his jeans, he fastened his gaze on his precious offerings and waited.

He'd told Mama he would go to the park today, like usual, and be home in time for his paper route. He pulled out his lunch. Mama had packed his favorite: two peanut butter and jelly sandwiches, potato chips and Orange Crush. Grinning to himself as the grape jelly squirted between the spaces in his front teeth, he thought of the story Mama told about girl-half and boy-half sandwiches. Today he would eat the girl-half of the sandwich first, the half with the curved sides.

As he ate, he remembered how he'd walked in the crisp morning air to the big grocery stores. No more stops at the corner market — not since the owner had run him off. Now it was just Apple Foods and Safeway. The boss men were nice there.

"Here you go, Billy Ray, take these to your critters," the man at Safeway had said, pressing packages of outdated food into Billy Ray's middle as though handing off a football for a big play.

Billy Ray had smiled and gripped the gifts, not daring to look down until he said, "Thank you." He had hurried from the store with his treasures and studied them outside by the bicycle racks.

Today has been a good day, he thought, as he sipped his soda and gazed at the cellophane wrappers rustling in the breeze. He liked the little whipping sound they made and the way the light bounced off them.

Then he reached into his jeans pocket and took out the pretty hair thingy. He stroked it gently and laughed out loud.

Chapter 4

Shuffling along the sidewalk, canvas bag bouncing against his broad back, Billy Ray tossed his newspapers. Sometimes he would pause to decide if a particular house was a part of his route; then he would continue along the street. He had been doing this route for three years, but sometimes he forgot a customer. *Boy, did Mr. Heisel get mad last week,* he thought.

"If you don't get the paper here in five minutes, I'm canceling my subscription!" Mr. Heisel had shrieked into the phone.

Billy Ray was thinking so hard he didn't hear the footsteps on the pavement behind him until a voice called, "Hey paper man, wait up." He turned to see his younger brother, Mike, loping toward him. "Hey Mike, how you doin'?" Billy Ray grinned and hoisted the heavy bag higher on his back.

"Not bad, Bro. Not bad. Hey, we've got to get going. It'll be dark soon. I see you didn't roll your papers before you left the house." Mike shook his head. "It's a lot easier if you do."

"Yeah, I was in a hurry," Billy Ray muttered.

"Come on, I'll roll and you toss." Grabbing a paper, Mike deftly rolled it and had a rubber band on it in an instant. Fifteen-year-old Mike was awkward sometimes, but mostly because his feet didn't seem to fit the rest of him. He did pretty well with his long fingers no matter what it was, dribbling a basketball or playing video games or rolling newspapers.

"All right, Mike," Billy Ray answered, happy to have help. They finished quickly, even with Mike's occasional clowning and Billy Ray's resulting confusion at what his brother was doing.

As they bounded the last few yards for home, Mike repeated the mantra he'd been telling his brother for as long as he could remember, "You're okay, Billy Ray, you're okay!"

*****

Gazing out the bus window, Kendra's eyes saw only the scenes of the past week. Two grown-ups had let her down when she'd tried to tell them about seeing Billy Ray with the barrette. She realized her last chance was her mother. But would Mom believe her? And if she did, would she be willing to go to the police?

Kendra thought back to another bus ride long ago when she had found a wallet under the seat. It held a lot of money — hundreds of dollars — the most money she'd ever seen in her life. She had wanted to keep it so badly. But she'd turned it in to the driver when she reached her stop.

Kendra had expected Mom to praise her for her honesty, but instead she had scratched at the chronic rash on her arms and yelled at her for being so stupid. "Why didn't you keep it? Wouldn't you like to have a few new school clothes and something besides crappy food to eat?" Mom had begun to cry and shake her head. Then she had sunk into a nearby chair and covered her face.

Kendra wanted to run back to the bus and start all over. It had been devastating to see her mom fall apart. Of course, Kendra wanted more clothes and maybe even some that didn't come from the second-hand stores. And the thought of trading their usual mac-and-cheese for a roast beef dinner with all the side dishes made her realize what a mistake she'd made.

When Mom had looked up moments later her face was calm, but there was a look in her eyes Kendra couldn't name. "Oh, I'm so sorry, honey. You did the right thing. It's just that sometimes I feel like we're so alone."

But her mom's words did little to take away the guilt she felt for failing her family. The bus lurched and Kendra's daydream evaporated as a woman fell into the adjoining seat and began talking. She was super friendly and talked so fast that Kendra had trouble following the conversation. The woman introduced herself as Peg Strong and launched into her adventures working as the office manager at a law firm. Happy for the distraction, Kendra became engrossed in the woman's stories.

Peg's eyes sparkled when she detailed her training routine for her first marathon in Boston. "I've really gotten into this thing," she said. "You've maybe heard how runners have more dirty shoes piled by the door than a farmer. Well, that's me."

Kendra laughed at Peg's remark. It made her think about how she was the best sprint runner in her gym class. But on the mile run, Kendra's classmates always overtook her long before the finish. Hearing how Peg started her training program four months in advance and gradually increased the mileage of her workouts made Kendra realize how she could build her own endurance and do better on the longer races.

She was definitely drawn to Peg. It wasn't just her gorgeous looks or her funny way of saying things, but she was really interested in her — Kendra Morgan. Peg asked about her school and friends, and what she liked to do in her spare time. So in the days that followed, whenever she was on the bus running errands for Mom, she'd watch for her new friend.

When Peg boarded the bus, Kendra would wave to the empty seat beside her. They'd fall back into the same easy conversation from the last time they'd met. Kendra found herself wanting to tell Peg more about her troubles, but she didn't know how to put it into words.

One day as the bus bumped along, Kendra stopped in mid-sentence as she glanced out the window and saw Billy Ray.

"What?" Peg asked as her eyes followed Kendra's. "Oh, do you know that man? Funny, I saw him in the park the other day."

"Yes. Well no, not really. I've seen him around here," Kendra stammered. Then before she knew it, she was pouring out the whole story about Cloud's death and Billy Ray.

When she finished, Peg asked, "Do you mean to tell me you think that man may have killed your classmate?" Her eyes were wide with disbelief and yet she was asking.

"I don't know, and I don't want to get him in trouble if he didn't do it," Kendra replied.

"I work at a law firm and this kind of information is just what the police need! It could be a real breakthrough. And just because Billy Ray had the barrette, doesn't mean he killed Cloud. The police are smart. They'll figure it out." Peg looked intently at Kendra for a response and added, "You've got to get your mother and go to the police. I'll go to the station with you, too, if you want."

A white wave of relief rushed through Kendra's body at Peg's words. Finally, someone who believed her!

*****

Lying in bed that night, Kendra thought about the day's events. She was exhausted and the scenes in her mind kept switching back and forth from the police station to home. Actually, reporting to the police had been easier than she expected. Even though the officers were big and imposing in their uniforms, they were gentle when they spoke with her and she found their questions easy to answer.

Of course, having Mom and Peg there had helped, too. The difficult part had been earlier in the day when she and Peg had to convince Mom to go with them to file the police report.

"Mom, this is Peg Strong, the lady I told you about that I met on the bus," Kendra said as she brought Peg into the apartment.

"Peg, this is my mom, Teresa."

"Hi," Teresa said. "Thanks for keeping Kendra company on the bus. It's good to know there's a responsible adult watching out for her. So what's going on?" Teresa looked from Peg to Kendra.

Kendra opened her mouth to speak, but didn't know where to start.

Peg came to the rescue, "Could we sit down? This is going to take a few minutes."

Teresa motioned to a chair.

Peg was well into what Kendra had told her about Billy Ray and the hair clip before anyone could draw a breath. As her story progressed, she would ask Kendra to fill in some relevant detail.

Teresa stared at them, a stunned look on her face. When Peg finished, Teresa drew a deep breath and said, "It's nice of you to take an interest in my daughter but sometimes she doesn't see things quite right, you know?"

Kendra could hardly believe her ears.

Peg leaned forward in her chair, "Teresa, this isn't about your daughter. I'm doing what I need to do. If there's even a tiny chance Billy Ray knows something about this case, we've got to report that he had Cloud's barrette!" Peg's normally brown eyes were nearly as dark as her black hair.

Teresa's bitter words hissed through a clenched jaw. "I suppose you're right, but I don't like getting friendly with the law. They haven't been especially helpful to me and my girls. My ex-husband does pretty much what he wants and the cops don't care."

Teresa glanced at Kendra and saw the hurt in her eyes. Her shoulders sagged at the sight of her daughter's disappointment. "But I guess that's another story." She seemed to release her anger with a huge sigh. "Oh, all right! Get your sister ready, Kendra, and we'll go down to the station."

*****

Yes, that had been the hardest part of the day, but now it was over. The whole long ordeal was finally done. Now she could go back to being the old Kendra. Then she realized she wasn't the old Kendra anymore. The new Kendra knew some things about people she didn't want to know and yes, some things she was glad to know. Maybe this was part of growing up. Whatever it was, she knew she would never be the same again.

Chapter 5

The next day was Saturday and Kendra was bursting to tell Audrey everything that had happened. Audrey had been slammed hard with the flu so she didn't know about Kendra's failed trip to the police station, her encounter with that slimeball, Brent, or her chance meeting with Peg, which led to Billy Ray being taken into custody.

"Meet me halfway. There's so much to tell you about!" Kendra whispered over the phone after she learned Audrey was well enough to go out.

"Sure, I can leave in a few minutes," Audrey's reply mirrored the excitement Kendra felt.

Kendra threw on her coat and raced out into the pale November sunshine. She was nearly to Audrey's house before they met. Grabbing her friend by the shoulders, she exclaimed, "The police took Billy Ray into the station yesterday. I met this woman named Peg on the bus. Oh, she's so nice, Audrey, you won't believe it. We went to the police. Even Mom went!"

"Whoa girl, you're going too fast!" Audrey looked bewildered. "The last I knew you were going to the police by yourself. Where'd this Peg come from? Start over again, would ya?"

Kendra took a big breath and began with the first incident outside the police station where she had chickened out, and worked her way to Billy Ray's being taken into custody. When she got to the part about asking Brent Grimsby for help, she faltered. Finally, she said in a low voice, "He tried to persuade me to — you know — have sex with him."

"Are you sure, Kendra?" Audrey asked. Her eyebrows arched sharply.

"I know it sounds nuts. At first, he said he'd help. The trouble was that he said he wanted something in return. He looked at me so strangely that I knew for sure what he was after. I got out of there as fast as I could. It really freaked me out. It still gives me the creeps." Kendra shivered and hugged herself.

"Ewww!" Audrey exclaimed.

"I wish I would've had the courage to tell him what a scum he is. And I know I should tell Mom, but I just can't. I'd be so embarrassed." She threw her arms in the air. "Anyway, she'd say I imagined it — I know she would."

Kendra wanted to change the subject. It made her uncomfortable talking about Grimsby even to her best friend. "I'll just stay away from him, no worries." She quickly continued on about getting to know Peg Strong. "It's not like talking to other grown-ups. She tells me stuff about her life, like she's a marathon runner. And she really listens to what I have to say."

"When we happened to see Billy Ray out of the bus window, I spilled the whole story. And she believed me, Audrey!" Kendra drew a breath. "I'm so relieved that Billy Ray's in custody. I hope he rots in hell if he was the one who murdered Cloud!"

"Me too!" Audrey exclaimed.

*****

Downtown at the police station, Billy Ray's meaty fingers clenched and unclenched as the two policemen questioned him.

Earlier in the day the officers had come to his house and handed his mama some papers. Then they went through his tidy bedroom, moving everything out of its place. All his belongings: the stack of video games, the packs of baseball cards and his ceramic animal collection, always so carefully arranged, were scattered everywhere. One of the men began pulling things from his dresser drawers and found the hair thingy with the bright stones.

The officer had held it in the air like a trophy. Turning to Billy Ray, he said, "Where'd you get this?"

When he couldn't speak, the man said, "We'll have to take you downtown now."

Mama had sat close to him in the police car, patting his leg and telling him everything was fine, but he knew it wasn't. When they arrived at the station, the men had walked him to a small room with a big window on one wall.

The officers had asked over and over again where he'd gotten Cloud's property. He had wanted to tell them, but the words flew away from him.

"Just tell them, Billy Ray. There's nothing to be afraid of." Mama said.

After awhile the men's voices had grown louder. The tall one slapped his big hand down hard on the table where Billy Ray sat. "Speak up, man! All you have to do is tell us where you got the damned barrette!"

Billy Ray had jumped and begun to shake from head to toe. He wanted to tell them, but he just couldn't. Somehow sitting here in this room made him feel he had done something very wrong. *This is where they bring bad people,* he thought. He shook his round head from side to side.

Finally, the men told him that since he wasn't cooperating, they would have to keep him overnight. They left him there without another word. It seemed like a long time before Dad and Mike had come into the room and scraped two straight-backed chairs up to the table.

"Billy Ray, I'm sorry that Mike and I couldn't get here sooner. We drove as fast as we could," Dad said. "Look at me. You've got to tell the police anything you know about the barrette or Cloud Nicholson."

Although he had spoken softly, the tone of his voice had made Billy Ray even more afraid.

"We know you didn't do anything wrong. Just tell the police whatever you remember. All right, son?"

Billy Ray had moved his lips to speak, but the only thing that escaped was a bit of saliva. It trailed down his chin. He wiped it away and lowered his head once again.

*****

Later that night, Mike returned to the police station. Dad had gotten special permission for him to spend some time with Billy Ray in his cell. Mike knew the cops' generosity was because they hoped his brother would tell him something about Cloud's murder. *Not that I'm not itching to know himself,* Mike thought. *Billy Ray does some pretty silly things sometimes, but he would never knowingly hurt anyone. Well, it doesn't matter; Billy Ray needs me and I'm just glad I can be here to make him feel better.*

"Wazzup Bro," Mike greeted Billy Ray. The tiny cameras placed in the corners of the cell weren't hard to spot but he doubted Billy Ray had noticed them, and he sure wasn't going to mention them.

Billy Ray sat up on his bunk. "Hey, Mike. Can you spend the night?"

"'Fraid not, but the people here will treat you right. Hey, wanna play some Crazy Eights?"

"I guess."

Mike pulled a deck of cards from his jacket, sat at the end of the bed, and shuffled them while Billy Ray concentrated on remembering the game. He watched the tension leave Billy Ray's face as the cards slapped gently on the blanket. Mike looked around the tiny cell at the peeling paint, the metal toilet and sink, and the bare walls. The echo of the guard's voice speaking to someone in the hall seemed muffled by the heaviness of this place. Mike felt suddenly afraid for Billy Ray.

After they had played a couple of games in silence, Billy Ray blurted, "I didn't hurt that girl, Mike, whatever her name was — Cloud — yeah, Cloud. Honest, I didn't hurt her."

"I know you didn't, man. Don't worry. Everything will be fine."

"I knew you'd believe me." Billy Ray sighed.

"'Course I do. You wouldn't hurt a fly, but jeez, how did you get her hair clip?" Mike reached across the table and nudged Billy Ray's hulking shoulder with the flat of his hand.

"Found it. Found it in that old man's garbage can. You know — that guy the kids are afraid of."

"Old Man Campbell?" Mike asked.

"Yeah."

"You know you aren't 'sposed to go through people's garbage! Don't you remember getting in trouble for taking food for your animals from the next door neighbor's trash?"

"Yeah, I know, but I saw those pretty stones sparkling in the sun right there on top of the yucky stuff, just winking at me." Billy Ray shrugged. "It was a bad thing I did, wasn't it?"

"Yeah — I mean, no. No, it wasn't bad. Sure, you shouldn't go through people's trash, but you can't go to jail for that."

"Oh." Billy Ray scratched his head.

Mike scooped up the cards. "I'll tell Mama and Dad and you'll be out of here by tomorrow morning. It's late now. You better get some sleep." He pushed him gently down on the pillow and gave him a hug. "You're okay, Billy Ray, you're okay."

Chapter 6

"I can't believe it!" Kendra exclaimed when she saw Audrey at school the following Monday. "My mom heard that they let Billy Ray go. The word around the neighborhood is that his brother got him to open up about what happened. Supposedly, he saw the clip in Old Man Campbell's trash and helped himself." Kendra grabbed her lunch and slammed her locker.

"Sounds like you aren't convinced Billy Ray is innocent." Audrey said. They settled in their usual spot in the corner of the cafeteria.

Kendra pulled her sandwich from her lunch bag and continued, "I don't know what to think, except the cops don't seem very good at their jobs. Mom said the gossip around town is that they have no suspects and the investigation is stalled. Maybe we ought to do a little snooping around on our own." Kendra leaned forward to look into her friend's eyes.

Audrey studied her friend's face. "You're kidding, right?"

"No, I've been thinking about it a lot! You know how goofy the police are."

"Not really, but I've got a feeling you're going to tell me." Audrey replied.

"You've seen it on TV. Tons of murders go unsolved, even with all the new technology like DNA, GPS, and brain fingerprinting."

"Yeah, I guess so, but what can we do that the cops can't? And what in the heck is brain fingerprinting?" Audrey asked.

"A suspect is shown pictures on a computer screen and the cops can tell if he knows about a crime by the way he reacts. He wears a special headband gizmo that measures electrical waves."

"I don't get it."

"First the cops show him familiar stuff and record how his brain responds. Then they show him photos of the crime scene and register his brain activity. They can tell by comparing the two results if he knows what happened. Pretty cool, huh?"

"Sometimes I wonder about you," Audrey shook her head.

"I just like finding out about this stuff," Kendra explained. "Anyway, we've got an edge because no one will suspect us of snooping. After all, the only things girls care about are boys and French fries, right?"

Audrey laughed. "Yeah, I've noticed how you go all pink in the face when Johnny Haskins talks to you."

Kendra giggled. "Isn't he a hottie?" Just the mention of Johnny's name made her flush from head to toe.

"Okay. Back to earth, girl. If we were to do something so completely nuts, maybe we should check out Old Man Campbell. He only lives a couple of blocks from me."

"Good idea," Kendra said. "I've heard other kids talk about him. They say he plays with dolls and talks to someone, even though he lives alone. But we don't know him. How do we get him to trust us?" Kendra glanced at the kids at the next table to be sure they weren't eavesdropping. She cleared her throat and continued, "Well, let's think about it. We could follow him to the corner market and pretend to bump into him, spilling his groceries. Then we'd help him pick them up and offer to carry them to his house."

"That wouldn't work. You know how grumpy old people can be. He might get mad and tell us to get lost," Audrey replied.

"You're right, he probably wouldn't go for that," Kendra said.

"I know! How about if we pretend we're running a yard service? I'm sure Dad would let me borrow the lawn mower." Audrey flipped her heavy auburn hair back like she always did when she knew she had a good idea.

"Sometimes you amaze me!" Kendra said. "When can we get the lawnmower?"

"You're really serious about this, aren't you? Okay, give me some time to work on Dad."

"Definitely," Kendra said. "And we need to be thinking about what we'll say to Old Man Campbell. We don't want to blow it. If he's the killer, it could be dangerous. But on the other hand, we could crack this case wide open." Kendra shivered with excitement at the possibilities of what lay ahead.

*****

Convincing her dad to let her and Kendra use the lawnmower wasn't quite as easy as Audrey expected.

"Audrey, this idea of starting a yard service with Kendra is a little more complicated than you realize," Mr. Worth said between breaths as he hefted weights overhead in his makeshift home gym. "It takes some planning. You'll need to keep records of your income and expenses. Have you and Kendra talked about how you'll split the profits?" He plunked the weights on the floor and climbed on the Stairmaster.

I should've known Dad would come up with this stuff, Audrey thought. *He's always looking for ways for me to 'learn about the world'.* "Oh sure, Dad, we know we have to keep track of everything and I figured we'd just split the money 50-50."

"If you want this to be a real business you should get a bigger percentage because you'll both be spending the same amount of time, AND you'll be providing the lawnmower. Or you could do less work, unless Kendra has some garden tools or wants to take on the paperwork aspect. That's the way real businesses are set up. The percent of ownership, or profit, matches the percent of contribution by the partners."

Mr. Worth was warming to the idea. "This could be a valuable experience for you, Audrey. Your first job and one that involves labor, materials and ownership principles," Mr. Worth huffed away on the stair machine.

"So does that mean I can borrow the mower?" asked Audrey, trying to hide what she knew was a deer-in-the-headlights expression.

"Yes, but first I want to see a written contract between you and Kendra on the terms and conditions of your business agreement."

"Sure, Dad." Audrey waited until the next day. She knew Dad would have filled Mom in on what she and Kendra wanted to do by then. Mom was always happy to help her only daughter. She even sketched out the business contract. "Here you go. You and Kendra will have to fill in the particular terms."

"Thanks, Mom. You're great," Audrey called as she ran out the door, agreement in hand.

At Kendra's apartment, they sat down at the kitchen table. "You know, this looks pretty good," said Kendra. "Maybe we should really do it." Audrey laughed, but Kendra continued, "No, seriously — I could use the money, but catching Cloud's killer takes top priority."

"Well I get an allowance, and physical work doesn't sound too great to me. Dad thinks it'll be a good experience for me though, so let's take this back home right now and see if he goes for it," Audrey said.

*****

The girls sat across from Audrey's dad in the living room.

"Nice work, girls. This is almost as good as some of the things I've seen at my CPA firm. You're welcome to use the lawnmower each Saturday." Mr. Worth's eyes smiled at them over the top of the contract.

Audrey and Kendra squealed with happiness and Audrey hugged her dad. Kendra said, "Thank you, Mr. Worth."

He grinned and announced, "Finchville doesn't know it yet, but it's got a couple of dynamo business women in the making."

Kendra's face flushed. "We'll do our best, won't we Audrey?"

Chapter 7

Not far away, a man looked out the living room window of his apartment. His foot tapped relentlessly on the soiled beige carpet. A teenage girl strode by in the deepening twilight. In the seconds it took her to pass, he noted all that she offered. Nice long legs beneath the dark stretch pants, thick honey-colored hair to mid-back. Her furry, hot pink earmuffs pulled at something in the pit of his stomach. They would be the first thing he would rip from her. *Entitled brat,* he thought. *She's probably got a different color for every day of the week.* Then he would relish the stiffness of her oh-so-tender body as she realized that what he would take next would be a much bigger deal.

If I want some pleasure, it's up to me to find it. If there's one thing I learned from Ma and Pa, it's that. Pa was such a goat, never standing up to anyone — especially Ma. Never lifting a hand to protect his little boy or himself. Well, I fixed that, didn't I?

Darkness had closed in when he looked down and saw his foot still hammering away at the unforgiving floor. *You dummy — get up and close the blind. Gotta have privacy. Makes life so much easier.*

A small smile played across his set lips. *Another young thing would be real nice. And the earmuffs something new for my collection. She'll come by again and I'll be ready. Oh yeah, oh so ready.*

Chapter 8

Old Man Campbell scratched absentmindedly at the thick mat of white hair jutting from his shirt top. He stared at the two girls with the Honda lawnmower standing at his door. Hair seemed to take a liking to him. Forests of it grew in his ears and on his eyebrows, even spreading down onto the base of his nose. Little white whiskers stood proudly there, as if they had every right to inhabit those old pores.

"Hi," Kendra gulped, trying not to stare at the whiskers. Her eyes dropped to his feet, shod in cheap plastic sandals...yellowed toenails and more hair. No help there. She swallowed hard. "We're from A & K Landscaping and we'd like to mow your lawn." She looked into his eyes, which were milky blue and blinking from the bright light. "That includes raking and trimming for just ten dollars," she hurried to add.

After what seemed like an eternity, he responded, "I reckon it could use it one more time before winter sets in. Usually do it myself, but the old arthritis is acting up again. Being out in the chilly air makes it worse." He looked them up and down. "You girls live close by here?" His gaze shifted to Audrey.

"I live over on Circle Drive, just a couple of blocks from here," Audrey said. "And we have a friend, Penny, who lives a few houses down." Audrey pointed in the direction of Penny's house. "She thought this street might be good for our business. A lot of big lawns."

"Oh, the Roberts girl. Yes, I know who she is." He nodded. "Just startin' out, huh? Well, I admire young people who want to work, but if you don't do a good job I won't pay what you're asking."

"No problem." Audrey said. She stooped to prime the mower and then gave it a yank. Kendra and Old Man Campbell waited expectantly. Two more hard pulls, a few sputters. Then a smooth roar brought a triumphant look to Audrey's face. "What are you waiting for, Kendra?" she called as she leaned into the mower's handle.

Kendra grabbed the weed whacker and fired it up with a flourish, saying a silent thanks to Audrey's dad for showing her how to handle the unwieldy thing.

Luckily, the girls had remembered Penny Roberts lived near Old Man Campbell, so they had quizzed her beforehand. Even though Penny didn't know him well, she knew Saturday was his day to play bridge. But she hadn't been sure of the exact time he left — just early afternoon. So Kendra and Audrey worked as slowly as possible, stealing glances at their watches whenever they could.

*****

For days before going to Old Man Campbell's house, the young detectives had argued about

Kendra's plan. Audrey had been dead set against going into the old guy's house while he was gone.

"That's breaking in and if we're caught, we could be arrested!" Audrey exclaimed.

But Kendra kept insisting it was the only way to find out if he was Cloud's murderer. Searching for some way to persuade her friend, she asked, "Would it make you feel better if we got a guy to go in with us?"

"Oh sure, I get it. You want to ask your heartthrob, Johnny Haskins." Audrey gave Kendra a knowing look.

As always, Kendra felt her cheeks grow hot when Johnny's name was mentioned. "He's the only one I think we can trust to keep what we're doing a secret."

"You don't know that for sure." Audrey said.

"I guess you're right about that." Kendra grudgingly admitted.

After many assurances from Kendra that the scary deed would take only a few minutes, Audrey caved from the pressure. "Oh all right, Kendra. I don't think I've ever met someone as stubborn as you!"

To reassure Audrey, Kendra had agreed they'd only go in if they could find an unlocked door or window. "That way if we get caught, we could say we heard a cat cry out and went in to save it," she said. Audrey had given Kendra her worst dirty look, but nodded in agreement.

A half hour into the project, Old Man Campbell stuck his head out the door and yelled over the din of the machines, "Can't you make those things go a little quicker?"

Audrey yelled back, "We're going as fast as we can!"

Old Man Campbell slammed the door. A little while later, he came out with car keys in hand. "Come back for your money tomorrow," he said gruffly. "I don't pay in advance."

As soon as he was out of sight, the girls shut down the machines.

"Look Audrey, the back window's open a crack," Kendra poked Audrey's side and pointed.

"Kendra, let's forget this. We could get in real trouble." Audrey's eyes darted furtively around the yard.

"I know you're scared. So am I, but what about Cloud? Doesn't she deserve some justice? Anyway, no one can see us back here." Kendra hoisted herself onto the edge of a rain barrel and through the window. "Are you coming?"

Audrey stared as her friend disappeared from view.

All was silent for a few seconds then, "Wait 'til you see this!" Kendra exclaimed.

Audrey's curiosity overcame her fear and she followed Kendra through the window. "Wow, Old Man Campbell needs a maid service more than a yard service," she whispered as she looked around the room.

"What's that smell?" gasped Kendra, "and why are you whispering?"

The kitchen table held stacks of papers, magazines, and the remains of a waffle breakfast, complete with waffle iron and crusted bowl of batter. Several pet food bowls sat on the cracked linoleum floor in one corner of the room. Remnants of semi-dried cat food clung to the bowls and the floor indiscriminately. Flies buzzed about, not seeming to mind that some of their feast was topped with fuzzy mold.

Pointing toward the corner with the bowls, Audrey said, "I think it's coming from over there. And I'm whispering because we shouldn't be doing this!"

"Let's look around and get out of here as fast as we can," Kendra said.

"I don't know why I'm stupid enough to let you talk me into these things. There's nothing here but filth," Audrey replied. "Oh, all right! But let's be quick. You search in here and I'll start in the living room. I've got to get away from this stink."

"Thanks a lot," Kendra muttered as she plugged her nose and began going through the papers on the table. Finding nothing there, she remembered hearing that old people sometimes hid things in the freezer or refrigerator. A check of the freezer revealed only half-evaporated ice cubes, and the refrigerator was nearly empty. Eggs, milk, and some unidentifiable leftovers made up most of the contents. A check of the cupboards and drawers produced the same results. Old Man Campbell had little food on hand. What he did have was a lot of junk. Apparently, he saved everything: rubber bands, newspapers, plastic containers, pencils, matches, corks, package ties, candles, and bits of soap.

She joined Audrey in the living room and they searched everywhere — even under the sofa cushions. Kendra wasn't sure what they were looking for, but she'd heard once that it was possible to tell a lot about a person by being in his home. *Okay house, what do you have to tell us?* But in spite of her silent question and the fact that they went over every square inch of the room, there was no clue Old Man Campbell had done anything wrong.

"I'll check out the bathroom real quick," Audrey said.

"Okay, I'll take his bedroom. We have plenty of time, but I'd like to get out of here," Kendra said. "I feel funny going through his stuff."

"So now you're growing a conscience," Audrey muttered.

The bedroom dresser produced only the expected items of clothing, but on a shelf in the closet Kendra found a cigar box with official looking papers and a medal on a faded ribbon. Old Man Campbell must have served in one of those long-ago wars. Then she came across a picture of a handsome young man in a uniform. It seemed incredible he was once so young. She looked at the picture more closely. Although his demeanor was solemn, there was a twinkle in his clear eyes and a softness around his mouth. For some reason, realizing Old Man Campbell was young once made him less scary.

Kendra's daydream burst when she heard a yell from the other room. She resisted the urge to run for the nearest door, and headed in the direction of the scream.

Audrey was clutching her chest in fright. "Oh my God! It scared me to death!"

"What?" Kendra demanded.

Audrey pointed wordlessly in the direction of the living room.

Kendra went to Audrey and squeezed her arm hard. "What scared you?"

"I think it was just a cat, but it flew out of nowhere! I heard a racket and saw a blur of yellow spring from behind that cabinet and zoom by me." The color was returning to Audrey's face. "That was pretty silly of me. Sorry if I scared you, too."

"Not to worry. I love to have my hair stand on end." Kendra grinned to hide the fact that she had been frightened, too. "Okay let's check the back room and then we're outta here."

What they found in the spare room raised even more questions in their minds about the man who lived in this house. It was chock full of dolls — dolls of all kinds and from all over the world. Most had a label describing where they were made and the date. Some even had an accompanying letter listing the original owner and more of the doll's history. Many were soldier dolls of various nations and wars.

They were preserved and protected by glass display cases. There was not a speck of dust anywhere; nor a cobweb, nor the clumps of cat fur prominent throughout the rest of the house. This room obviously claimed Old Man Campbell's special attention. "Wow, I guess Penny was right about him playing with dolls," Audrey exclaimed.

Although they wanted to stay and examine the dolls more closely, they were afraid of being discovered. Checking to be sure they'd left everything just as they'd found it, they exited through the same window they'd entered. After big sighs of relief, they headed towards Audrey's with lawn equipment in tow.

"Well, we didn't find any incriminating evidence," said Kendra. "What we do know is that he's a war hero. The doll thing is kind of creepy though, don't you think?"

"Totally. Also, he's poor," Audrey added.

"How do we know that? Maybe he eats out a lot," Kendra countered.

"I went through his desk. His checkbook had only a little over a hundred dollars in it. Looks like he gets by on what the government sends him, which according to my dad isn't enough for a gnat to live on. Also, he had wet clothing hanging in the bathroom. He doesn't have a washer or dryer or, come to think of it, even a clothes basket lying around the place. He must do his laundry by hand to save on expense," Audrey finished.

"Weird!" Kendra said.

Audrey continued, "Also, Penny said she spied on him one time when he was on his porch. He talks to his cats like they're people. One day she heard him say, 'Okay, Bubba, you want a treat?'"

"Penny swears the cat jumped on a little three-legged stool and sat up like a dog! Then Old Man Campbell gave him a treat. And you won't believe this next part."

"What?" Kendra asked.

"The old guy said, 'What do you say?' And the cat actually meowed really, really loud. Then he said, 'Good job!'"

Kendra laughed at the thought of Old Man Campbell performing circus-type tricks with his cat. "So is he a suspect, or just a funny old man?" she asked more to herself than to Audrey.

"He seems odd, but so do my grandparents sometimes," Audrey replied.

"Maybe we need to get to know him better. It's a good thing he didn't pay us yet. Gives us an excuse to go back," Kendra said.

"At least we won't have to haul the lawn equipment with us. This stuff is heavy." Audrey grunted.

Chapter 9

Knocking on Old Man Campbell's door the next afternoon, Kendra and Audrey wondered if their plan to find out more about him would work. "Hi, Mr.Campbell. We came back to collect for the lawn. Nice day, huh?" Kendra asked.

"Probably one of the last warm days we'll see for a long time. The weatherman says snow's coming at the end of the week." A huge yellow feline snaked around his ankles.

"Oh! Who's this?" Kendra asked, bending to pet the well-fed animal.

"That's Bubba. Guess he likes you."

Kendra sat down on the wide porch step. Bubba walked over and flopped lazily on his side next to her. "I don't think I've ever seen such a huge cat."

Audrey joined Kendra on the porch and bent to scratch behind Bubba's ear. "He's so-o-o-o soft," Audrey added.

"Yeah, I guess I'm gonna keep him. Had him 'bout ten years now," the old man said as he settled in a rocking chair. His porch was like many in Finchville — big enough to host a party. "Got another one here somewhere. Name's Mandy. She's a Himalayan — a lot shyer than this guy."

"I hope she comes around while we're here. I'm crazy for cats," Kendra said.

"Well, we can sit a spell and see if she shows. You girls did a real nice job on the lawn." He handed Kendra a crisp green bill.

"Thanks Mr. Campbell. Now that winter's almost here and shoveling snow isn't our thing, we were thinking we would start a house cleaning service. Would you be interested in having some of your chores done?"

Old Man Campbell chuckled. "I think the Housekeeping Fairy must have sent you. The place hasn't had a good cleaning since my wife passed." Then a hint of a frown flickered across his hairy brow. "I'd have to wait a few weeks though, first of the month when my check comes."

Kendra thought fast. "No problem. In fact, Audrey and I are offering a free sample of our service as a way of getting new customers. We'll clean one room of your choice at no charge."

"Sounds great. The kitchen needs it the worst. Why, I've plumb forgotten what color the countertop is."

Kendra and Audrey gave each other knowing looks, and they all laughed together.

"We could get started right now if you want," Kendra offered, "unless you need us to bring our own cleaning supplies."

"No, got everything…but do your folks know you're going into the cleaning business?" He scratched his stubbly chin. "You know I live alone. I'll give you my phone number so your parents can call me. Yeah, especially with the terrible thing that happened that Nicholson girl. Yup, better have 'em call me first."

"Okay," said Kendra, "we will." Her heart skipped a beat at the mention of Cloud's name. She wanted to follow up, but hesitated. *Best to get to know him a bit better,* she thought.

Just then two chocolate-brown paws and a beige face framing a chocolate-brown mouth peeked over the edge of the porch.

"Oh, there's the other one. Here kitty. Here kitty, kitty, kitty," called Kendra.

"Yup, that's Mandy, my little girl. Pretty, isn't she?"

"Oh yes! Here Mandy, here girl," Kendra called. The chocolate-brown ears twitched, the round blue eyes blinked. Effortlessly, the feline leaped to the porch and padded over to meet the newcomers.

"You are gorgeous," Kendra said.

Mr. Campbell smiled and leaned back in his rocker while the girls fussed over his pets. It turned out he liked to talk. He was full of stories — mostly about Bubba and Mandy — but some about himself and his wife, who had died a year ago of heart disease. A good share of the afternoon slipped away before he handed them his phone number and said goodbye.

As they walked home, they agreed there was no way the old guy would hurt anyone. "Maybe the cops told him something about the case that would help us though. Penny told me he has some connection to the police department," Audrey said. Suddenly the significance of their offer to clean Old Man Campbell's kitchen hit her. "Oh, brother! Now I've got to sell Dad on another deal and this one's going to be harder. He never lets me go in strangers' houses," she moaned.

"You've got to convince him! Now that we're getting to know Old Man Campbell, I think it would be easy to get him to talk about Cloud. He even brought her name up today," Kendra pleaded. "Please try, Audrey! You've got to try."

"Okay, okay — I'll give it my best shot," Audrey conceded. "You know, you're lucky. Your mom doesn't check up on you as close as my folks do."

"Yeah, she's got enough on her mind."

"What do you mean?" asked Audrey.

Kendra was silent.

Audrey prodded, "What, Kendra?"

"I don't like telling friends this stuff," Kendra said.

"Why not?"

"When they find out what my family's like, they disappear."

"Hey, good friends have each other's back. Just like when you took the rap for Cloud in Mr. Thomas's class," Audrey replied.

Kendra's gut told her that Audrey wasn't the kind who would judge her. *It would be so great to have someone to confide in about what goes on at home,* she thought.

She drew a breath and plunged into what felt like a huge confession. "My dad's a drunk. A mean, violent drunk. He follows us from place to place and makes our lives miserable."

Kendra rushed on, "Every so often, he sobers up and persuades Mom to take him back. Mom got preggie with Toni during one of those times. Dad's supposed to help her with child support — what a joke! She doesn't make much at the café even though she works a lot of hours." She shrugged her narrow shoulders.

"Cranky, tired and worried about how we'll get by — that's Mom. What I'm up to is the last thing on her mind."

"That's too bad, Kendra. I didn't know." Audrey wanted to ask Kendra more about her dad being violent. But she felt so bad for her friend that for once, she was speechless.

Chapter 10

As it turned out, it wasn't as hard as Audrey thought it would be to convince her dad to let them clean Old Man Campbell's house.

When she approached him at breakfast, he responded, "Mr. Campbell, over on Columbus Street? He's friends with your Grandpa Worth. They served in the Navy together and they're still buddies after all these years."

"So you'll call and tell him it's all right?" asked Audrey, trying to hide her surprise at her unexpected good fortune.

"I wondered what you girls would do when you discovered the lawn service business was played out for the season. You've come up with a good alternative, but you're too young to be going into people's homes. Besides, I don't want your homework to suffer. I'll call him, but his is the only house I want you to clean."

"Sure, Dad. We'll start up the lawn service again in the spring." Audrey breathed a big sigh of relief.

*****

The following Tuesday afternoon found the detectives looking more domestic than sleuth-like.

"How do you get ahold of something, wearing these crazy things?" Kendra complained as she struggled to pick up a penny from the wet floor with rubber gloves. Finally, in exasperation, she yanked them off and flung them in the direction of an overflowing trash can. It was almost suppertime and they'd been hard at work since school ended.

Mr. Campbell had started out watching them from his chair at the kitchen table, rambling on about Bubba and Mandy. He soon realized he might be enlisted to help, and excused himself to the living room.

The kitchen looked a world better and they were nearly finished, but their backs ached and their stomachs growled.

Thank goodness Audrey's mom lent us kneepads, Kendra thought as she kneeled to finish the floor. Even so, her knees still hurt. It was such a slow process, having to scrub so hard and sometimes use a putty knife to scrape bits of food from the tile. She kept reminding herself this hard work could eventually give them some clues to solving the murder. She ran the events of the case through her mind as a diversion from the hard work. *Wouldn't it be cool if the cops found the killer's DNA on Cloud's hair clip?* Rousing herself from her daydream, she said, "I'm never going to think housework's easy again."

"No kidding," said Audrey, pushing her hair from off her flushed face as she washed the front of the cabinets. "I'm giving my mom a big hug when I get home."

As they prepared to leave, they realized they'd forgotten the oven. "Oh no," Kendra cried. But then she brightened and whispered, "Maybe it's a good thing. It'll give us an excuse to come back so we can talk. We were too busy this time."

"Couldn't we just skip the oven? This sucks," Audrey complained. When Kendra didn't answer, Audrey knew it was no use arguing.

They found Old Man Campbell dozing in his recliner, reading glasses perched on his whiskered nose. Mandy, the Himalayan, peered at them from beneath the newspaper on his lap. Mr. Campbell's eyes fluttered open when they entered the room. "My, it's funny how this happens to me. One moment I'm reading the newspaper and the next thing I know I'm waking up." He took off the glasses and yawned. "You girls all done?"

"We didn't get to the oven, but we'll be back tomorrow," Kendra said.

"Well, let's take a look." Slowly he lifted Mandy from his lap and walked to the kitchen. He inspected the refrigerator and noted the sparkling table, counters and floor. "You did a terrific job, ladies! Gonna have to call you 'ladies' now 'cuz you work as hard as any grownups I know."

Kendra and Audrey beamed.

"The oven will be all ready for you. I'll put some of that stinky cleaner in before you get here. Don't forget to bring your rubber gloves, ladies." He held the door open and bowed low in mock humility as they passed by him.

Kendra rolled her eyes. "Yeah, wouldn't forget them for anything. See you tomorrow, Mr. Campbell."

On their way home, Kendra told Audrey about her idea that the cops might find some of the killer's DNA on Cloud's barrette. "That could crack the case," Kendra said.

"Wouldn't that be great? I'm sure Old Man Campbell didn't kill Cloud, but I'd sure like to know who did," Audrey replied.

"Me, too," Kendra said. "I can't wait to go to the old guy's house tomorrow to see if the cops told him anything about the case. I hope Penny was right when she told you he has an in with the police."

In the gathering darkness, a hooded figure appeared across the street. He loitered just out of the beam of the street light. Kendra grabbed Audrey's arm and whispered, "Look! Who's that?"

"I can't tell," Audrey replied, "but let's get out here!" Hand in hand, the girls ran for home.

Chapter 11

As Kendra and Audrey labored through the deep snow, the only sound Kendra could hear was her own heavy breathing. Winter had come quickly and ferociously, hurling a heavy blanket of snow over the town and blowing banks of it against whatever stood in its way. It hardly seemed possible that only days ago they'd been mowing Old Man Campbell's lawn. The storm had continued throughout the night. Now all that remained were dry flakes floating from tree to bush, like tiny birds.

A gray, spent sky looked down on the small, quiet town that seemed smaller and quieter than ever. Dreading the thought of the long, cold days ahead, most of the citizens of Finchville were hunkered down in their cozy homes.

Kendra saw a lone figure in the distance. The woman was making surprisingly good headway through the drifts, her head down and body bent forward. Determination seemed to be propelling her along. As she neared, Kendra realized it was Peg.

"Audrey, there's Peg Strong, the woman who helped me."

"Oh, yeah?"

"I've wanted you to meet her. If she hadn't happened along I might still be trying to get someone to listen to me about Billy Ray."

When she was within speaking distance, Kendra called out, "Hi Peg. What are you doing here?"

"Oh hi, Kendra! The bus I take home from work decided to detour through a snow bank." She laughed breathlessly. "Fortunately, my condo's only a few blocks away," she said, motioning with her gloved hand.

"This is my friend, Audrey," Kendra said.

"Hi there." Peg greeted Audrey with a smile. "Are you two on your way home, too?"

"Not yet," Kendra said. "We're going to Mr. Campbell's house. His trash can is where Billy Ray found Cloud's hair clip."

"How could I forget that? But why are you headed there?" There was a note of concern in Peg's voice.

"At first we thought Mr. Campbell might be the murderer, but now we feel bad we ever suspected him. He's been very nice to us, and it turns out Audrey's family knows him."

"Yeah," said Audrey, "we're thinking maybe the police gave him some information. We're going to ask him about it."

"That's highly unlikely. They're not supposed to give out details on an open case," Peg said. "Kendra, I know I encouraged you to go to the police, but it sounds like you're getting way too mixed up in this. Let the police do their job. Okay?" She stamped her feet in the snow.

Kendra looked off in the distance. "Yeah, you're probably right. We'd love to talk more, but we better get going before we turn into icicles."

"Don't go over to Mr. Campbell's, okay?" Peg called over her shoulder as she tromped away.

"We won't, Peg," Kendra answered. The girls turned and resumed their slog through the snow.

"Peg seems nice, Kendra. I can see why you trusted her to help with telling the cops about Billy Ray."

"Yeah, I feel terrible lying to her just now. But we can't let on how involved we are. You heard her reaction. Do you think Old Man Campbell will discourage us, too?"

"Probably. But we can't give up. Like you said before, the cops don't seem to be doing anything."

"We'll have to be sneaky then." Kendra said. They fell silent, both girls lost in their own thoughts.

Arriving at Mr. Campbell's, they peeled off snow-logged boots, coats, scarves and gloves and left them on the enclosed back porch to dry.

"You girls like a little hot chocolate before you declare war on the oven? I was just gonna have a cup."

"Yes, please," Kendra and Audrey replied in unison, and laughed at their simultaneous outburst. Sitting with Old Man Campbell at the kitchen table, the girls warmed their hands on the steaming mugs and chatted about the first storm of the season. After a time, they all agreed they were in for a long, hard winter.

"Yup, don't think Bubba and Mandy will be going outdoors much," predicted the old man. "Especially Mandy. She thinks snow is a terrible inconvenience."

"Really?" asked Audrey.

"Yeah, winter of '03, I don't think she came out of hiding 'til the groundhog did," he chuckled.

Well, here goes nothing, Kendra thought. "Mr. Campbell, the other day you mentioned Cloud Nicholson."

"Yes, I'm sure you girls heard what happened to her," he replied.

"Yeah, everyone in town knows. Plus, she was a friend of ours," Kendra said. "We're really upset about it, and want whoever did it caught."

"I agree with you there, that's for sure," he said, sprinkling more marshmallows in his cup.

"We heard the police found some evidence here. Is that true?" Kendra asked.

"It is. In fact, I was a suspect for a while. The poor girl's hair barrette was in my trash can. But I was over in Hanford the night of the murder and I had plenty of folks that vouched for me. Thank goodness, or I could be in the clink right now."

"We're glad that didn't happen. We wouldn't have met you then," Audrey replied.

"It was very scary, realizing how quickly your whole life might change. Right away, I thought of Bubba and Mandy and wondered who would take care of them if I was sitting in jail."

"Well, besides being great landscapers and housekeepers, we're wonderful pet sitters," said Kendra. "If you ever need to be gone for a while, we'll gladly take care of your babies, no charge."

"That's mighty nice of you, but I'd never leave them overnight. At least, not willingly." He chuckled.

"Mr. Campbell, did the police tell you anything about the case? Do they have any clues?" asked Audrey.

"No, I don't think so. They called a few days after their visit and said they'd ruled me out as a suspect."

"Too bad. Not that they ruled you out, but that you don't remember anything else. Kendra and I have been trying to figure out who the killer could be," said Audrey. "Every time I think of Cloud and that I'll never see her again, I'm just so sad."

"Me, too," said Kendra. "Sometimes when I'm doing something as simple as making popcorn I think, 'Cloud will never get to do this again.'" Kendra looked into the old man's milky blue eyes and into Audrey's large brown ones, and exclaimed, "It's not fair — it's just not fair!" Her own eyes smarted with tears.

"I sure wish I could help." The wrinkles on Mr. Campbell's high forehead deepened as he handed Kendra a tissue. "Wait a minute. I overheard something about checking out a lead of some kind." He scratched his head and stared off into space. "Now what the devil was it?"

The girls waited in silence, fearful of breaking his concentration.

"Oh yes, that was it," he muttered to a speck on the wall. "As they were leaving, one detective told another to meet up at the house in Lancaster where Cloud was at her cousin's birthday party with her brother before she went missing. Sounded like they were planning to interview more family members there."

"Wow — we did hear something about a party, but didn't know any details!" Kendra said.

Audrey and Mr. Campbell could see Kendra was lost in thought. Then her face brightened. "Audrey, isn't your brother, Tyler, friends with Cloud's brother?"

"Yeah, but my brother isn't always friends with me," mumbled Audrey. She looked at Kendra's earnest expression. "I know what you're thinking, Kendra. Forget it."

"Thanks, Mr. Campbell, you've been a ton of help," Kendra said. "We owe you. Do you like pie?"

"Is the sky blue?" he asked. "Seriously, I want this person caught as much as you do." He bent to pet Bubba. "I don't need any reward, but you girls aren't going to do anything foolish, are you?"

"Oh, no way! We just want to know what's going on with the case." Kendra changed the subject. "Hey, would you care if we came by this weekend after your card game? We love hearing your stories about the cats."

"Sure, come on over," he said.

Audrey picked up on Kendra's cue to divert Mr. Campbell's attention. "We better get to work if we're going to be home before dark," she said. She jumped up and carried the hot chocolate cups to the sink while Kendra donned the hated rubber gloves and tackled the food-caked oven. As they worked, their minds whirled with new possibilities for their investigation.

Chapter 12

"Ty, you're pretty good friends with Cloud's brother, aren't you?" Audrey asked as she walked into her family room.

What?" Tyler asked absentmindedly, his gaze fastened to the TV set.

"Josh. Josh Nicholson. He hangs with your group of friends, doesn't he?" Audrey persisted.

"Yeah, so what?" he replied.

"Well, I was wondering if you could do Kendra and me a big favor."

"Like what?" he glanced at Audrey, then back to the football game.

"Kendra and I are trying to find Cloud's killer. We need more information about her last day." Audrey tried not to sound too anxious; she was positive a real detective would be very cool in this situation. At the same time, she wondered for the umpteenth time how she could let Kendra talk her into this stuff. "All we know is Cloud and Josh went to their cousin's birthday party in Lancaster and she never came home. We need a lot more info like the address of the party, the time they got there and left, who was there — you get the idea."

"Ha!" Tyler exhaled. "You're kidding, right? First, why should I help you, my kid sister, who devotes herself to making my life miserable? And second, Josh isn't talking about Cloud." He unwrapped his long legs from a yoga-like position and swung around to face Audrey at the end of the sofa. "How in the heck do I even bring her name up, much less ask him a million questions about the day she died? You must be nuts."

"You could figure out a way. You've always been good at getting people to talk. Remember the time Jay Thornton knew the phone number of that girl you liked, and you tricked him into giving to you?"

"How'd you know about that?" He tossed a pillow at her. "No, you aren't going to fool me like I fooled Jay. Forget it. FOR...GET...IT!"

"Okay, but I may have to tell Dad about a certain incident with the car," Audrey said.

"You wouldn't! You little creep!" He rolled off the sofa, pulling his shoes on. "See what I mean. You do nothing but make me miserable. I'm outta here!" He slammed the door behind him.

Audrey called after him, "We need to know ASAP, Ty!"

After Ty got over being irritated with Audrey, he thought about how much he'd like to stop the person who had ravaged Cloud's body so horribly. He knew that in the end he'd do whatever he could to help find the murderer of his good friend's sister. *I'll talk to Josh when he's in the right mood. Besides, I don't want to look too jazzed to help Audrey. She might get ideas and expect it all the time. No, I'll be laid back about it.*

Chapter 13

She hasn't been back. The girl with the hot pink earmuffs. Dammit! She had been passing by in the late afternoon almost every day. He'd rearranged his furniture so he had the perfect view from his recliner. He could see all the way to the end of the block. As soon as she appeared, he'd slip out the door. The tall hedge next to the sidewalk would be perfect cover for him to hide behind while she approached. But he'd have to move fast. His hand closed around the rag he planned to use to stifle her screams.

It was past dusk, and with no further hope of seeing her tonight he reluctantly rose from his chair and stumbled to his bedroom closet. Setting his beer can aside, he slid a cardboard box out and lifted the lid. *Oh yes, baby.*

His latest victim's things were on top. He pulled her blue sweater out and quickly unbuttoned his shirt. Dropping to the bed, he clutched it to his bare chest. The old familiar yearning began to uncoil in his belly. It spread through his body like fire.

Good thing I saved a few things. I wish I would've kept the pretty hair thingy and some of her other stuff. This sweater's wicked good though. It's so soft! Just like her skin was. He clutched it to his face and inhaled deeply. *Yes! I can still smell her!*

Rolling to his side, he abandoned himself to the gnawing hunger in his gut, his new prey temporarily forgotten.

Chapter 14

Sunlight filtered through the checkered curtains onto the top of Kendra's sister's blonde head as she bent over her Pokémon coloring book. Toni's chubby fingers clutched the orange crayon as she concentrated on her work. Mom had asked Kendra to watch Toni while she did the weekly shopping. Kendra didn't mind, especially since she had a project of her own.

Audrey had called with information about the day of the murder. As Kendra's mind spun with the details, she realized she needed a way to sort out her thoughts. She grabbed her spiral notebook and sat beside Toni at the kitchen table. Gazing at her sister without seeing her, Kendra jotted down the sequence of events surrounding Cloud's death.

Mon., Nov 4	Cloud's body found
Sat., Nov 9	Saw Cloud's hair clip in Billy Ray's pocket; tried to tell Mr. Thomas and Brent Grimsby, but a big nothing there
Fri., Nov 15	Went to cops with Peg; Billy Ray Houston taken into custody
Mon., Nov 18	Audrey and I learn that Billy

	Ray found the clip in Old Man Campbell's trash
Sat., Nov 23	Searched Old Man Campbell's house, but no clues
Tues., Nov 26	Old Man Campbell tells us Cloud went to a birthday party with her brother the day she died
Fri., Nov 29	Audrey's brother, Ty, tells us: The party was a family get-together at Cloud's Aunt Laura's house…645 Sycamore St. in Lancaster. Party was for Cloud's older cousin, Brittany…sweet sixteen

Ty had learned that Josh and Cloud had arrived at the party about 7:30 p.m. The house was filled with relatives, neighbors and Brittany's friends. The big scoop was that Josh and Cloud had an argument, and Cloud rode back to Finchville with her Uncle Frank. She asked her uncle to drop her a few blocks from home. That was about 9:30 p.m. She wasn't seen alive again. Two questions plagued Kendra: *what did Josh and Cloud argue about, and was Uncle Frank telling the truth?*

"Look Kendra, isn't it pretty?" Toni asked, extending her picture.

"Yeah, that's nice, Toni. Are you going to do another?" Kendra replied with enough interest not to disappoint the little artist.

"No, only Pikachu. He's my favorite," she announced emphatically. "I wanna watch the Muppets now."

While Miss Piggy and Rowlf entertained Toni, Kendra phoned Audrey to go over the details. "Do you think we can get Old Man Cam…you know…I don't like calling him that anymore, I'm going to start calling him Mr. Campbell. I know the other kids at school call him that, but it doesn't seem right. He's a good guy."

"Yeah, you're right. Totally," Audrey agreed.

"Anyway, do you think he'd drive us over to Lancaster? I'd like to know more about what happened at the party, and especially this Uncle Frank guy."

"I doubt it, but okay, let's talk to Old – I mean Mr. Campbell when we go to see his doll collection tomorrow. Bring your notes, too," Audrey added.

*****

The following day was sunny but frigid. Kendra wrapped her long scarf over her nose and mouth to keep out the stinging cold and tramped over the packed snow to meet Audrey. Turning a corner, she realized an old Toyota pickup truck had slowed and was driving alongside her. She looked at the driver, and her heart sank.

"Kendra, honey," her dad yelled as he pulled over to the curb, "where 'ya going?"

Kendra kept walking. "To meet a friend." She barely glanced his way, but noticed he was clean-shaven and his brown curly hair neatly trimmed.

"No time for me, huh?" he asked gruffly. The intensity of his look bore through her.

"Are you going to see Mom?" She hated herself for asking, but had to know.

"Yeah, come on — we'll ride over together." He waved her toward the truck.

"Don't ask me to do that," she said as a wave of panic rushed over her.

"Well, it's great to know my own daughter doesn't trust me," he shouted as the truck's tires squealed away from the curb.

Kendra's knees felt rubbery. She remembered the time Dad had picked her up from school when she was seven and took her to an unfamiliar family. He told the woman who lived there that Mom knew Kendra was with him. For days she'd wondered if she would ever see her mom again. As time passed, her hopes dwindled. But somehow Mom found the house and came to get her while Dad was at work, avoiding an ugly confrontation. Once she was safe at home, Kendra couldn't believe she'd actually gone to school and not told a soul that her dad had kidnapped her. *Well, I was young then,* she thought. *I know better now.*

Lost in thought, she didn't see Audrey until they were nearly nose-to-nose. "Oh hi, Audrey! I just saw my dad."

"You did? I didn't know he even lived around here."

"He doesn't. I'm not sure why he's here." What she really wanted to say was her dad was on one of his sober streaks and trying to reconnect with her family. But no words came.

"Hmm," said Audrey. She started to quiz Kendra about their meeting, but seeing Kendra's clenched fists, she stopped and changed the subject. "Oh, did you remember your notes? I think we should go over the whole thing with Mr. Campbell, except for the parts about him, of course. He wouldn't be too happy if he knew the whole story." She giggled a little. "Anyway, he might think of something more if we review the case."

Kendra felt lucky to have a friend like Audrey who could make her forget her troubles. Almost, anyway. "Yeah, I'm glad we've got him to help," she mumbled.

Knocking on Mr. Campbell's door, they heard him call, "Come on in, girls. I'm in the back — thought I'd straighten up a bit before you got here." They found him carefully rearranging a billowy, taffeta dress on one of the German dolls. "I picked this one up when I was overseas, but most of them were my wife's. Some even came from her mother." His voice trailed off as though remembering something far away. His smile failed to hide the sadness in his eyes.

He must be very lonely, Kendra thought. "She's beautiful," she replied. She meant what she said, but her voice held more enthusiasm than she really felt. Seeing her dad was ruining her day.

"I'd go back to playing with dolls if I had one like her," Audrey agreed.

"Yes, the German dolls are definitely the pick of the litter. France and Italy turned out some fine ones, too, but they couldn't figure out how the Germans got the porcelain skin coloring so real."

Mr. Campbell proceeded to show off his collection and indeed, it was spectacular. There were priceless and one-of-a-kind dolls. A few were of little value, like the troll and plastic Betty Boop dolls. Most were very old; many were from other countries and cultures, and several had personal letters accompanying them. The letters told fascinating stories about the dolls and their previous owners.

There was a ragged cloth doll that had belonged to a slave's daughter on a plantation in Virginia. It was roughly sewn from heavy cotton and yarn, and the letter with it told how the girl's mother had sewn it by candlelight. And there was the lovely French doll with tightly wound black curls, red-pursed lips and a flowing satin dress that had belonged to a girl whose family managed a seaside resort in France.

After they examined each doll, Kendra said, "Mr. Campbell, we got some information about the day Cloud died, and there are a couple things that are bugging us. Could we talk about it?"

Mr. Campbell looked surprised, but said, "Sure, let's go in the kitchen."

They sat around the kitchen table and Kendra filled him in from her notes.

"Hmm. Interesting. It's good you're keeping a written record. I know detectives keep journals for their cases. What else can you tell me?"

Kendra told him how her efforts to turn Billy Ray in were ruined every time until she met Peg Strong. When she mentioned her encounter with Brent Grimsby, she called him a creep.

Mr. Campbell's considerable eyebrows shot up. "Why do you call him that?"

Kendra felt her face growing hot.

Audrey came to the rescue. "He said some stuff to Kendra — tried to convince her to do something bad in return for his help in reporting Billy Ray to the cops."

"Is that right?" The old fellow scratched his whiskered chin. "Tell you what. I'll take a little trip over to Lancaster and see what I can find out about the argument and this Uncle Frank. It does seem strange that he'd drop Cloud off a few blocks from home instead of taking her to her door."

"Could we go with you?" they asked simultaneously.

He laughed. "Sometimes I think you two are twins, especially when you say the same things at the same time." He shook his head. "It's not a good idea for you to tag along. I'm sure your folks would get upset if they heard about you playing detective. I'll go over while you're at school tomorrow, and give you a full report when I get back."

Kendra and Audrey knew better than to argue. "Sure, Mr. Campbell," Kendra replied.

Chapter 15

The gravel road to Lancaster lay like a gray ribbon between the snow-covered fields. It was mostly free of snow, but there was still enough to keep the gravel from hitting the underside of the car. In the summertime, driving on the roads around Finchville sounded like the inside of a popcorn kettle. Ivan Campbell liked the quiet. It gave him time to think.

He was relieved he didn't know Cloud or the rest of the family personally. It would've been too hard to ask the questions that needed asking. *A very ticklish business for sure. Hate to cause them more pain than they've already suffered,* he thought. Assuming Cloud's cousin would be at school this morning, he hoped to find Cloud's aunt at home and willing to talk to him.

He took a deep breath and said a silent prayer that he was doing the right thing as he pulled up to a big house with an even bigger lawn. It was like many of the homes in this prairie country: a white two-story with a front porch spanning the width of the house. A German shepherd rose from his bed by the front door, hackles rising on his back. His top lip curled back to reveal needle-sharp teeth.

Ivan couldn't help but think *this is the perfect excuse for me to forget this whole crazy thing,* but a visual of Kendra and Audrey mourning their friend urged him from the car.

He approached slowly, extending his hand as a peace offering. "Hi, Champ. How's it goin'?"

The dog came off the porch and advanced just as slowly toward the stranger. He sniffed the back of Ivan's hand and in seconds his handsome coat settled back into place. Man and dog walked together over the narrow path cleared through the snow to the front door.

At his knock, a plump woman greeted him. "Morning. What can I do for you?"

Clearing his throat, he sputtered, "Good morning. My name is Ivan Campbell and I'm from Finchville. Do you have a minute?"

"Campbell from Finchville? Okay, I'm listening." She sounded cautious.

He cleared his throat. "Well, if it wouldn't be too troublesome, I'd like to ask a few questions about your niece, Cloud. I take it you're her Aunt Laura?"

Her face froze at the sound of her niece's name and she started to close the door.

"Oh, please wait, Mrs. Nicholson! I know this is forward of me, but Cloud's friends from school are terribly upset about what happened to her. I've met two of them — Kendra Morgan and Audrey Worth. They're fine girls and when they asked me to help, I couldn't turn them down. I was so hoping you'd understand." He turned his broad-brimmed hat round and round as he spoke.

Through what was now a slit in the door, Laura studied his face. Then she noticed her dog sitting comfortably beside the stranger and laughed softly. "I can see Webber trusts you. I guess that's good enough for me. He's got more insight into people's character than most folks I know."

She swung the door open. "No sense heating the outdoors. Come on in. I was just going to have a cup of coffee. Would you like one?" She shook her head as though questioning her snap decision, but led the man through the house anyway.

Hardly believing his luck, Ivan followed her into the kitchen and sat where she directed him. "Animals and I get along pretty darned good. Fact is I've never met one I didn't like," he said.

As she poured two steaming mugs and settled herself across the table from him, he noticed the yeasty aroma of bread rising. An unexpected wave of longing for his wife flooded over him.

"The way I look at it is, we all have to stick together through these bad times," Laura said. "Cloud was a beautiful girl with her dark hair and eyes. Hardly ethereal like her name, but earthy and so full of life! Of course, her parents are still horribly devastated. Our neighbors and friends have been so supportive, helping us however they can."

"I lost my wife a ways back and I know what you're saying. We can't do it alone. Just now, when I came in here and smelled the bread dough rising, I missed her all over again. She was a whiz in the kitchen and the best wife a guy could ever hope for."

"You and I have something in common. My husband died in an accident five years ago. I still miss him, too."

"Sorry to hear it." Ivan shook his head.

"We were well into middle age when we had our daughter, Brittany. It's been tough raising her alone. Well, I could go on about that forever, but let's get to the reason for your visit."

What a fool I was to come here, he thought. He frowned down at his coffee. "I'm embarrassed to say it, but Kendra and Audrey have this crazy idea that we can help find Cloud's killer. I've never been the kind to meddle and here I am doing it, and with a perfect stranger, too! I'd best be leaving." He began to push back from the table.

"Oh no you don't — I don't think it's crazy at all! There are cases on *Dateline* that are solved with the help of family and friends all the time." She jumped to her feet and dipped into a cookie jar disguised as a Holstein cow. "I've made these molasses cookies and I'd hate to see them go to waste."

Ivan cleared his throat and tried to ignore the heat in his cheeks. "Well, all right. If you're sure it won't dredge up too many unhappy feelings, I'd like to ask about the birthday party. We're hoping we might discover more clues for the police."

Laura pushed the plate of cookies toward him. "Go right ahead. Ask away."

He took a gulp of coffee and plunged in, inquiring about Cloud and Josh's argument on the night of the party.

"Oh, it was just a typical brother-sister spat. Something about Josh getting a body part pierced. Cloud said if anyone in the family was going to get a piercing, it would be her. She was very competitive with her brother, that's for sure."

"So it wasn't anything serious?"

"No, not at all! Overall, it was a fun party for everyone. My daughter said it was her best birthday yet. Of course when we learned later that Cloud didn't make it home, that all changed." She shifted in her chair. "What else would you like to know?"

"Just one more thing." He hesitated. "This is very awkward to ask. Hope you don't take offense, but I understand Cloud's Uncle Frank was the last person to see her...."

"Oh, no! Frank would never hurt her!" Laura exclaimed. "I've known him since I married his brother 38 years ago. Couldn't ask for a better man. He loves kids. My gosh, he's worked at the Boys and Girls Club forever. "

"I'm sure you're right. I just had to ask. You know how it is when you have a mystery. You go through and eliminate suspects and motives, etcetera." Ivan let out a deep sigh of relief and wondered how convincing he sounded. He felt like a darned fool.

"Of course," she said graciously. "Have a cookie, Mr. Campbell."

Drawing courage from her response, he threw in one last thing. "Anything else you can think of that might be helpful? Sometimes even the smallest thing can turn big."

"No, believe me. I've played it all out in my mind a million times!" she exclaimed.

He took an enormous bite of cookie. "Would it be okay to call you if anything else comes up?"

"My number's in the phone book."

They talked on for awhile about the weather and such and when he left, she tucked a parcel of cookies beneath his arm.

He had one more stop to make before heading home. Even though he believed Laura Nicholson trusted her brother-in-law implicitly, he knew that people didn't always know their loved ones as well as they thought.

The creaking '74 sedan came to rest in Jack Huffner's driveway. He and Jack went way back to Navy days. After their service in World War II, Jack had gone to work for the Finchville Police Department. Of course, he'd been retired many years but he still had connections. As Ivan got out of the car, he saw him shoveling snow from the sidewalk. "Hey there, don't you know you're too old to be doing that?"

Jack straightened and pretended to toss the snow shovel at Ivan. "Okay, you better take over."

They laughed, shook hands, and clapped each other on the back. "How are you, old timer?" Jack asked.

"Better than you," Ivan replied. More chuckles.

"Well, I suppose you won't go away without a cup of something hot, so come on in. I didn't want to wrestle with this snow anyway."

*****

Driving home, Ivan was happy with what he'd accomplished. Jack was going to ask his cop buddies to check for any criminal record on Frank Nicholson. Frank being a director at the Boys and Girls Club could be a red flag. And most importantly he thought, *Laura didn't know why he hadn't taken Cloud directly home.*

"Hi, kids. Dad's home. Wait 'til you hear what I did today." He grabbed the Whiskas treats from the kitchen shelf and rattled the bag. As always, Bubba raced to greet him while Mandy remained aloof on her perch in the window alcove. "Met a darned nice-looking woman over Lancaster way, and then stopped by Jack's."

As Ivan poured out a couple of cat treats, he thought of the man who had tried to force himself on Kendra. "Oh, hell! I forgot to ask him to run a background check on that Brent Grimsby character, too." He put down the box of treats and walked to the phone.

Chapter 16

"Hello," Kendra mumbled into the phone.

"It's 9:30 and you're still in bed? We're going to Mr. Campbell's today; it's Saturday, remember?" Audrey's voice jarred Kendra awake.

Suddenly alert with excitement, Kendra replied, "Oh yeah, I sure hope he has some news from Lancaster. I'll meet you there." Looking around the quiet apartment, she wondered where Mom and Toni were. Padding into the kitchen, she found a note telling her they'd gone grocery shopping. As she grabbed an old-fashioned donut, she wrote her own quick message:

I'll be with Audrey today. Call you later.
Hugs,
K.

Pulling on her sweater and black pants, Kendra realized she wanted to tell her mom all that was happening. Her life had changed so much in the last few weeks, she hardly felt like the same person. But their family had always been secretive.

Dad's drinking and Mom's bruises weren't talked about in the light of day. Only in the dark of night did she learn anything. She must've been about four when she became aware of Mom calling Dad a no-good frigging drunk. She learned to dread the times Dad left with his friends, knowing he'd return barely able to stand. She would pull the pillow over her head to try to shut out the yelling and the sound of slaps and moans and mysterious thuds.

One night after one of Mom and Dad's fights, he had staggered into her room. She held her breath fearing he would hit her, too. Instead he shouted an obscenity as he crashed into a wall. It took Kendra several minutes to grasp that he was so drunk that he thought he was in the bathroom next to her room.

She pushed the awful memories from her mind. No, she couldn't tell Mom about their investigation. If she got an "A" on a paper or if Toni said something cute, sure. But nothing important. Definitely not anything about feelings. Their family didn't talk about real stuff.

Arriving at Mr. Campbell's, she found Audrey hunched against the cold on the weathered porch step. "He's not here. I'm just dying to know what he found out."

"Me, too." agreed Kendra. "Well, we've got the whole day. What should we do now?"

"He could be anywhere. Any ideas?"

"Let's ask the neighbor, Mrs. Peerman. Mr. Campbell says she's so nosey, she knows when something's gone bad in his refrigerator from five hundred feet." They went into one of their giggling spasms as they crossed the street. A drapery moved at the picture window, sending them into another round of laughter.

Putting on more serious faces, they knocked at the door. It swung open to a woman with sharp eyes and eyebrows growing straight back at an angle to her hairline. Her face reminded Kendra of a bald eagle she'd seen on the Discovery channel.

"Yes?"

"Hi. We were wondering if you've seen Mr. Campbell lately. We thought he'd be home this morning."

"And who are you girls?" Her sharp eyes grew sharper yet.

"I'm Kendra Morgan and this is Audrey Worth. We're friends of Mr. Campbell's."

"Oh, really? Well, I guess I have seen you over there once or twice," she conceded. "How did you get to know him?"

"We have a yard and cleaning service. Mr. Campbell hired us," Kendra answered.

"And what do you want with him today?" she asked.

Talk about the third degree, Kendra thought. "Oh, nothing important, sorry we bothered you." She turned to leave, tugging at Audrey's elbow to follow.

Mrs. Peerman called as they retreated down the sidewalk, "All I know is he came home pretty late last night and left again early this morning. Not like him to go anywhere on Saturday mornings. Usually doesn't leave the house 'til his bridge game in the afternoon. A bit strange, I'd say."

"What an old witch!" Kendra whispered. "But I feel better knowing he was home from Lancaster last night."

"I wish he had a cell phone so we could check with him," Audrey said, pulling her own from her pocket. "Since he isn't here why don't we call Peg, the woman that helped you? Maybe she'll have some ideas for digging up information."

"Not a good idea," Kendra said. "Remember how she told us to stay out of the investigation?"

"Have you got a better plan?" Audrey challenged. "We'll convince her Mr. Campbell's doing all the legwork, and we're just passing information to him."

"Oh all right, but we've got to be very careful with what we tell her," Kendra relented.

"Siri, call Peg Strong in Finchville, Nebraska." Audrey instructed her phone.

Peg picked up and agreed to meet them at Arbor Square in the Tortoise Shell Café for lunch. "That's perfect since I've got shopping to do there and I want to talk to you girls anyway." Her tone sounded urgent.

Jogging to the bus stop to keep warm, they joked about how they should have Mrs. Peerman on their detective team and speculated about why Peg wanted to talk to them. Bus 55 delivered them to the mall in what seemed to be a long fifteen minutes.

As they walked to the café tucked between The Gap and Victoria's Secret, they noticed the huge Christmas tree signaling Santa's presence at the center of the mall. A long, curling line of parents and small children waited ever-so-patiently to see the jolly old fellow.

"Do you ever wish you were young enough to believe in Santa Claus?" Kendra's eyes lingered on the scene.

"Huh?"

"Oh, I don't really want to believe in Santa again. It just seems like since this thing with Cloud, I'm different. I feel like something's missing, something more than Cloud. Do you know what I mean?" Kendra pulled at her scarf.

"Yeah, I think so. It's like the world isn't the same anymore," Audrey answered.

"Yeah, like we're not kids anymore."

"Hey, I'm not ready to be a grown-up yet." Audrey laughed and shoved Kendra toward the café.

Peg was already seated and checking out the menu. They chatted with her about everyday things until the server had taken their order. Then Peg got right to business. "Have you heard the latest?"

"What?" the girls said at the same time.

"A man accosted a girl in Newton."

"What do you mean, 'accosted'?" Kendra asked.

"Accosted...bothered...molested."

"That is so freaky!" Audrey shuddered and folded her arms tightly across herself.

"What happened?" Kendra asked.

"The word going around my law firm is that the girl was at the movies and her friend had gone to get popcorn. A man sat down beside her and started talking to her. Then he put his hand on her leg! The girl was so scared that she forgot all about her friend and ran home to tell her parents." Peg looked from Kendra to Audrey, and added as an afterthought, "The family is talking about suing the theater owners." She shook her head in disbelief.

"Wow! Do you think it was the same guy that killed Cloud?" Kendra asked.

"I know you want to solve the case, and it's got me worried," Peg said, ignoring Kendra's question.

"If only she'd told someone there instead of running for home. They might have caught the creep on the spot," Kendra said.

"She must've been so wierded out," Audrey said. "I wonder what the guy said to her."

"I'm sure the police questioned her thoroughly." The cords on Peg's neck were beginning to stand out as she talked. "Anyway, I wanted to warn both of you. Newton's only five miles away from here. I'm sure the police will catch whoever's responsible. In the meantime, be super careful and don't go looking for trouble." She took a gulp of water while the server delivered their sandwiches. "Now what did you two have on your minds?"

"Well, I guess it doesn't matter now. We wanted to fill you in on what we know about the case and see if you had any ideas." Kendra spoke with her head down, not daring to look Peg in the eye.

"You bet it doesn't matter! That's why I wanted to tell you about the Newton incident. I was afraid you were still playing detective. You could be kidnapped, tortured, and murdered! You don't want me to go into greater detail, do you?" Peg's voice was shrill.

"We understand don't we, Audrey?"

Audrey nodded.

Kendra squirmed a little in the booth, and then decided to chance more of Peg's anger. "But maybe you'll change your mind when you hear this; we have a helper — Mr. Campbell."

The girls told Peg the latest details and how Mr. Campbell was interviewing Cloud's family in Lancaster.

Peg put her head in her hands. "I *am* relieved to hear you have another adult involved, but you really don't understand the danger. You're probably lying to this guy like you lied to me."

"No way, Peg. We're only giving Mr. Campbell any information we hear, and he checks it out," Kendra said.

"Did the police release the Newton girl's name or age?" asked Audrey.

"You just don't get it, do you?" Peg exploded. "I suppose you would contact her next, if you could." She grabbed the check and her purse. "I've got the feeling you two are going to do just what you want. You're forcing me to call your parents!"

"Oh no!" cried Kendra. "We promise we won't do anything stupid! Please?"

"I'll call you later," Peg said over her shoulder as she hurried from the café.

On the way home, they mulled over their talk with Peg. They agreed they wanted the name of the girl in Newton, but the prospect of Peg calling their parents suddenly seemed much more important. Finally, their fear of being discovered drove them to a more pleasant topic...the Winter Wonderland Dance at school.

"You <u>are</u> going, aren't you?" Audrey asked.

"I guess so. I've never been to a dance before," Kendra replied.

"Neither have I. Do you think the boys will ask us to dance?"

"I hope not," Kendra mumbled.

"Why?"

"I don't know how." She shrugged.

"Well, come on over and I'll show you. It's lots of fun."

"Really, you can teach me?" Kendra squeaked in surprise.

"Really. Who knows? Maybe that smokin' Johnny Haskins will ask you to dance."

Kendra giggled and ran up the Worth's front steps, through the door and down the hall to the family room fast on Audrey's heels. Audrey was the only one she had told about her crush on Johnny. *He is so cool,* she thought.

"Lucky Ty's not here. He'd be a nuisance right now," Audrey said. She chose a song with a slow beat and began swinging her arms to the rhythm, shifting her weight back and forth. Taking Kendra's hands, she closed her eyes and swayed from side to side.

Kendra kept her eyes open, concentrating with all her might. Audrey began moving her feet, pulling her friend along with her. Kendra felt like a toy soldier, awkward and stiff.

"Loosen up. Go with the beat," Audrey said.

Kendra stopped for a moment. She listened to the music. She remembered what Mrs. Norbert, her music teacher, had said about hearing the rhythm in the music. There was a definite beat. One, two, three, four, one, two, three, four. She stopped thinking and felt the core of the song — the beat. She didn't have to do anything; just let the rhythm move her.

"That's it. You've got it!" Audrey exclaimed.

"Yeah, I think I do." Kendra smiled as she moved back and forth to the music.

"You're so bad, Kendra," Audrey said as she admired her friend floating around the room on her own.

Audrey's mom stuck her head in the door. "Are you girls having too much fun to stop for a snack?"

"Sounds good, Mom. You, Kendra?"

"Yeah, sounds great." Then she whispered to Audrey so Mrs. Worth wouldn't hear, "Afterward, we can try Mr. Campbell again."

When the girls did call there was no answer, even though they let it ring a long time. If they had known how their elderly friend was spending his day, they would've been very surprised.

"Okay, we can't wait around forever, Audrey. Let's go talk to Cloud's Uncle Frank before the afternoon's gone. Of course, we can't just blurt out what we want to know, but maybe we'll get some clues anyway."

"I don't know, Kendra. He could be dangerous." Audrey shook her head.

"It'll be okay. What can he do in broad daylight?"

"Well, maybe — but we've got to think of some excuse for going there so he doesn't know we're considering him a suspect," Audrey added.

"Come on, I know just the thing," Kendra reassured Audrey. "If we hurry, we can catch the next bus." It had been a no-brainer to find Frank's address. He was listed plain as day in Finchville's phone book. And the girls were pleased to learn he only lived two blocks from the bus stop. But when they arrived, no one answered their knock at the door. They heard the thudding sound of an ax splitting wood, and followed the noise down the long driveway. Behind the house, they found Frank Nicholson.

Although the day was so chilly that his breath was visible in rapid bursts, sweat shone on his sinewy forearms and brow. He paused as he caught sight of them in his peripheral vision and lowered the ax to his side. "Howdy. What can I do for you?"

"Hi." Kendra said, standing very close to Audrey. She knew she should make some kind of small talk, but the sun's glint on the head of the ax made her quiver inside. "Sorry to interrupt, but you're Cloud's Uncle Frank, right?"

At the mention of Cloud's name, Frank's face hardened.

"She was a part of our posse at school, and we'd like to ask your opinion on something," Kendra blundered along.

He lifted his worn Red Wing boot to the chopping stump and pulled a rag from his back pocket. He stared steadily at them as he mopped at the sweat running down his face and neck.

"We wondered if it would be okay to plan something at school in her honor, like a plaque or something. Do you think the family would like that?"

His strong jaw went slack, his eyes blank. He pulled his hat off and ran a trembling hand through his hair. "Get out of here!" His voice was guttural, hardly human.

Even though they could barely make out his words, there was no mistaking his meaning. Kendra and Audrey wheeled and hurried away.

"That didn't go well," Kendra mumbled.

"He's a very scary guy," Audrey replied.

Once they were safe on the bus, Kendra asked, "Well, what do you think? Does his reaction to a perfectly innocent suggestion mean he's guilty?"

"I think so, but maybe he's just feeling guilty 'cuz he was supposed to take Cloud home and didn't."

"Yeah, you might be right. I got so involved in thinking he might be the killer, I forgot about his feelings if he wasn't. Pretty stupid of me. But I don't think we can rule him out," Kendra said.

"Oh, I'd give anything if we hadn't gone there," Audrey lamented.

"Me, too. If he didn't kill Cloud, he was the only one who might know why Cloud wanted to walk the last few blocks home. And he sure isn't going to tell us now."

"Yeah, I wonder if Cloud was hooking up with a guy? Someone she didn't want her parents to know about?" Audrey mused. "Remember that older boy she was talking to in the corner of the cafeteria one time? He was obviously jacked up on something."

"You and I wouldn't dare get mixed up with some dude like that. But Cloud was fearless," Kendra said.

"Plus there were people who didn't like her," Kendra added. "There was the school computer incident…and remember the time she found out the combination to Butch Ladke's locker and left a dead rat underneath his gym clothes? I can still smell it!"

Audrey laughed. "Cloud definitely had a way of getting on people's nerves."

"But she didn't deserve to be killed," Kendra declared.

Chapter 17

The beeping of the alarm startled Ivan. *Why is that blasted thing tearing a hole in my eardrum? Oh yeah, I'm heading over to Lancaster again today,* he thought. Climbing out of bed, he stumbled to the kitchen. He bent to pour Friskies Senior Diet into the cats' bowl and felt the familiar painful catch in his lower back. *Wouldn't be right if I didn't have a few pangs at my age. A good, hot soak will loosen things up.*

Hanging his worn terrycloth robe on the back of the bathroom door, he filled the tub and tossed some clothing into the steaming soup. While Ivan bathed, he looked at his underwear and shirt floating in the suds. "Good Lord, I'm turning into an eccentric old fool," he said aloud. "Anyone seeing me wash myself along with my laundry would think I'm deranged."

A bit shaken at this insight, he realized this had been his habit since his wife died. He rose from the tub, dried off, and gazed at his face in the mirror over the bathroom sink. He felt unusually happy this morning, even with his discovery that he might be a bit odd. Raising an eyebrow, he turned his face from side to side, scrutinizing what he saw there. He clucked his tongue and spoke to the reflection. "You may be a little daft, boy, but good-looking just the same." He reached into a drawer for the tweezers and began plucking the bristly hair sprouting atop his nose.

On the way out of town, he angled the car into a parking space at the north end of the mall. From the oversized bells on the light standards in the parking lot to the gingerbread house scene in the Macy's window display, the colorful trappings of Christmas were everywhere. In recent years such things seemed superficial, but today they buoyed his good spirits even more.

He'd been meaning to spruce up his wardrobe for a long time, but it hadn't seemed important until today. Sauntering into the Men's Department, he selected a few items. At the encouragement of the young sales clerk, he added a couple of Tommy Hilfiger shirts. One was indigo blue — his favorite color. He'd never even heard of the brand before, but she assured him they were very fashionable.

He emerged from the fitting room in the Hilfiger blue shirt and a pair of gray slacks and said, "Could you cut the tags from these? I'd like to wear them."

"Certainly," the girl replied as she rang up his purchases. "You look very smooth! Thank you for shopping at Macy's, and come back after Christmas; we'll have more wonderful sales."

Ivan beamed at her compliment. "If you say so," he said.

*****

It was late morning by the time Ivan turned his car onto the street where Laura Nicholson and her neighbor, Bud Lone Tree, lived. By interviewing someone who wasn't a family member, he hoped to get an objective version of the people and events at Brittany's birthday party.

The man's little house sat back from the street. Near the front door, a carving of a bear's torso rose from an oak stump. Smoke hung low around the chimney in the still, cold air. At the side of the house, Ivan glimpsed a man with dark hair flowing over his shoulders. The man smiled and called, "Hey, you Mr. Campbell by any chance?"

"Yeah, that's me, all right. Call me Ivan."

"Come around here. Just bringing some wood in for the fire." Bud held the back door open with one arm, and balanced three logs in the other. "Laura told me you might stop by." He glanced at the leaden sky. "Looks like we're in for a storm before long." He pointed to an easy chair. "Sit down. Don't know how much help I can be. It was just a birthday party for Brittany. Nothing exciting."

Ivan lowered himself into the chair. "I understand. Laura didn't think anything unusual happened at the party either. And she's certain Cloud's Uncle Frank is beyond suspicion. But I'd like to hear what you have to say about it." He already felt comfortable with this man who filled the small room with his bulk.

Bud knelt beside the fireplace and prodded the sputtering flames with a poker. A large German shepherd lay by the fire; his tail thumped lazily a couple of times, but he showed no inclination to move. "I don't know if I'd go so far as to say Frank's above reproach." Bud hesitated a moment. "I've heard some things about him being into some questionable stuff on the Internet. You might want to check it out."

"Like what?" Ivan sat straighter in the chair.

Bud rose and gazed at his guest. "That's all I want to say about him. The Nicholsons have been my friends for a long time. I worked with Bob, Laura's husband, before he died in the accident at Winfield Metal. In fact, Bob's the one who helped me get this house."

"No problem. I would like to hear about that accident though." *Can't blame the guy for being loyal,* Ivan thought as he looked around the room. He noticed more animal carvings on a smaller scale than the bear in the front yard. Even though they were less than ten inches tall, they were skillfully detailed. Ivan was especially drawn to a sly coyote loping along a grassy prairie, his head down to catch the scent of prey. *Maybe this man is a sly coyote himself,* he thought. Then he immediately squelched the idea. There were some people you knew were okay the instant you met them. Bud Lone Tree was one of them.

"About four years ago, Bob was working in the warehouse and a load of parts fell and crushed his chest. Took him right in his prime." Bud frowned as he remembered the traumatic event.

"Yeah, I recall hearing about it. The safety commission had a big investigation," Ivan nodded.

"For what it's worth, it's a lot safer place to work now." Bud scratched his dog's head. "Doesn't make up for losing a friend, though."

"No kiddin'," Ivan agreed. "Say, your dog sure looks like the one I saw at Laura's yesterday."

"Same litter," Bud replied.

"That right? Nice animals, both of them."

"Thanks. Well, like I said, I can't think of anything out of the ordinary happening at the party. I was just happy for Brittany, turning sixteen and growing up so fine, even without her dad. They've both missed him a lot. And now losing Cloud — they're strong for white folks."

Ivan smiled at Bud's description. "I reckon they are. You Pawnee then?"

"One hundred percent. Lived on the reservation 'til I moved here."

"Do you happen to know if Laura's dating anyone?" Ivan studied his veined hands.

Bud's eyes widened and his nose spread across his face as he grinned. "Oh, so the murder isn't the only thing you're interested in?"

"Well, it didn't start out that way. I didn't plan on asking you that; it just popped out. To tell you the truth, this whole day has been rather strange from the get-go." Ivan plucked an imaginary thread from the sleeve of his new shirt. "Anyway, she's a terrific person — strong, like you said."

Bud nodded and didn't say anything for a moment. "I don't think she's dated anyone since her husband died, but why don't you stop by and ask her yourself?"

"I just might do that. Nice talkin' to you and thanks for your time." Ivan rose and headed for the door. Knowing he'd found an honest man, he wanted to ask more about Frank; but he knew once a guy like Bud stated his mind, only a fool would push him to change it.

*****

Knocking at Laura's door, Ivan hoped she wouldn't mind another impromptu visit. He needn't have worried. As soon as he saw her smile, he stopped fretting.

"Why, hello there! Did you stop by to talk to Bud today?" Laura straightened her blouse and smoothed her hair.

"Yup. Already been there. Met your dog's sibling, too." As she held the door for him, his heart bumped against his ribs so hard he thought they might break.

"Oh yes — Webber's littermate. I think there were eight pups and of the whole bunch, this one and Bud's were the best looking and the smartest. Of course, I may be a bit biased." Webber wagged his tail at the mention of his name and followed Ivan into the house.

"Got time for coffee or tea?"

"Can't stay long, but tea does sound good," he replied.

While Laura placed two mugs in the microwave and pulled teabags from a canister, he sat in the kitchen nook and tried to look nonchalant with Webber stationed at his feet.

"He definitely likes you," she said approvingly.

"Yeah, animals seem to know I'm an easy mark." Ivan stroked the dog's massive head, relaxed a little, and launched into a monologue on his favorite subjects — Bubba and Mandy. After a time he finished with, "They let me pretend I'm the boss, but we all know the truth."

Laura laughed. "That's cats for you. They're definitely in charge and it sounds like those two are no exception."

"Well, I didn't mean to go on so long. I just wanted to stop by to tell you thanks for the cookies.

Also, thought you'd like to know I have a friend — an ex-cop — doing some research on the case."

"That's wonderful, Ivan. As I said yesterday, we can't have too much help. I told Brittany about what you and Cloud's friends are doing. She thinks it's great, too."

"If you like, I'll give you regular updates." He seemed to be searching for the right words. "In fact, how would you like to meet Bubba and Mandy sometime?"

"You mean, come to your place?" Laura frowned.

"Sure. You could come and visit my kitty kids." Seeing her hesitation, he added, "I'll invite Kendra and Audrey, too. I know you'll like hearing about the way they've gone after Cloud's case like nobody's business." He added, "I've got my wife's old doll collection you might be interested in seeing."

They looked at one another and laughed. Laura curled her hair behind her ears and Ivan felt his heart flutter once more. "Why, that almost sounds like a date!" She paused briefly. "It also sounds delightful."

"Five o'clock on Thursday, then?"

"Absolutely." She leaned across the table and patted his forearm.

Chapter 18

Tiny, hard snowflakes drove like miniature nails into Kendra's face as she hurried home after the unfortunate scene with Cloud's Uncle Frank. She and Audrey had agreed to call Mr. Campbell the next day since he still wasn't answering his phone. Running up the steps, she hardly noticed the snow beginning to collect in the corners of the landing. It took a moment to overcome the shock of what she saw when she burst through the door. Dad was sitting with Toni on the sofa, with Winnie-the-Pooh propped between them.

"Well, there you are. I was hoping you'd get home soon," Dan Morgan said. His face brightened.

"Is Mom in the kitchen?" Quickly hanging her coat on a hook in the entry, Kendra turned towards the sound of pans clattering.

"Wait a sec — can't you visit a minute?" He leaned forward as if to get up, but sat back again.

"I'd better see if Mom needs some help with supper." Her breath came in gasps.

"How's school, honey?" he said. His voice was pleading.

His clothes were clean and pressed. *Still sober,* she thought. Kendra wanted to lift Toni from the sofa and run with her into the growing storm and away from this madness. Instead, she looked at her sister's little legs sticking straight out in front of her and hurried to the kitchen.

Kendra knew Mom had talked to Dad a couple of times since the day he'd followed her in his truck, but she had blocked it all from her thoughts. Keeping focused on finding Cloud's killer made it easy to forget. *Well, he's not going to charm his way back into my life like he's done so many times before.*

She stood next to her mother at the stove and hissed, "What is *he* doing here?"

Her mom looked down at the gravy she was stirring with such concentration she might have been performing major surgery. "Your dad's staying for supper. That's all. Set the table, okay?"

"Mom, you know how this always ends! Why do you do this? You're making a nice meal for him and he's got a restraining order saying he's not to come near us!" Kendra wanted to take her mother by the shoulders and shake her.

"He's your dad. He's Toni's dad. You can be decent to him for an hour, can't you? He's in a program and doing well. As long as he stays straight, it'll be all right." She raised her head and looked at Kendra with that look that said, *drop it.*

Kendra bit her lip. Her eyes stung like her cheeks had a few moments ago in the gathering storm. She didn't know how she could eat a bite. Her stomach was full of hate. *Sure — Dad could be charming, but charm didn't heal bruises or buy groceries.*

"Mommy, can I have more mashed 'tattas?" Toni asked. Sitting across the kitchen table from Kendra, she alone was enjoying the family meal. She chattered on about Christmas toys. "Will Santa still come if there's a lot of snow?" Her fair eyebrows pulled together into a frown.

"Santa's used to a lot of snow where he lives," Dan replied. "I'm sure it won't slow him down." He tried a couple more times to engage Kendra in conversation, but she either answered in monosyllables or not at all. The two adults seemed to have little to talk about besides the weather and his new job at the Honda distributorship. He talked about the size of his sales territory and how he'd soon have enough in commissions to help out with their bills, plus some Christmas shopping.

His eyes met Teresa and an unspoken agreement seemed to pass between them. He turned to Kendra. "I don't know how to say this. I've said it so many times before. I'm quitting...." His lips were moving, but no sound came out. He scrubbed his fingers through his curly brown hair and cleared his throat. "Oh dammit, never mind! I'm not going to say it. I'm just going to show you. You'll see." He wiped his mouth hard with his napkin. "Kendra, I don't expect anything from you — trust or forgiveness or anything. But someday, you'll know I'm not all bad."

Kendra stared stonily back at him and without a word, rose and went to the kitchen for Toni's mashed potatoes. *I can't wait for this meal to end,* she thought. *I'm not sure who I hate more — Dad or Mom. By the sappy look on Mom's face, I can see she's falling for his story all over again. Well, I won't! He's not ever going to con me again.*

As soon as he finished eating, Dan said, "Well, better get going. Thanks for the supper, Teresa — real tasty." Rising from the table, he nodded at Kendra and bent to kiss Toni on the cheek. He slipped into his parka. As he opened the door, large, damp snowflakes careened in, melting the instant they hit the floor.

"Looks like you're leaving none too soon," Teresa said. Her green eyes had a soft look Kendra hadn't seen in a long time. "Drive carefully, okay?"

None too soon is right, Kendra thought. She bolted toward the privacy of her bedroom. But Mom was on her heels, saying, "I understand how you feel, Kendra, but I think he really means it this time."

Kendra could scarcely believe her mother's words. "Oh Mom, he's never going to change! How many times has he promised, only to let us down again?"

Teresa scratched at the rash on her arms. Her eyes filled with tears. "I know. It's not fair to put you and Toni through this again. I'll make you a promise: if he blows it, we'll move someplace where he'll never ever find us. Okay?" She put her hands on Kendra's shoulders and looked at her sadly.

Kendra wanted to cry out, *But he always finds us and you always give in. We've only been here less than a year. I just start making friends and we have to pack up and go. I'm sick of running and being afraid.* But her mother looked so small and alone, she could only turn her back and stare out the window at the white fury engulfing them.

*****

Kendra woke the next morning to discover over a foot of snow. As she squinted out her bedroom window at the blinding brilliance, she wondered what good the sun did. There was no warmth in it. It only made her eyes ache to look at the vast world of white. A snowplow slowly graded mounds of the stuff to the side of the street. It seemed intent on burying the parked cars as it inched down the street. There were already snowdrifts of three feet or more where the wind had blown its cold deposits against buildings and cars.

The sound of the television drew her to the living room where she found Mom and Toni watching the local news. The blizzard covered over half of the state. Vicious winds, heavy snowfall, and low temperatures had caused one death already, and the meteorologist was warning listeners to stay indoors. "Well folks, you know what they say about our wind: 'One day the wind stopped blowing in Nebraska, and everyone fell down.'" He chuckled and shook his head. "This one was a little worse than it needed to be, though. If you must go out, take extra care."

"Good thing it's Sunday. Looks like we'll be staying in today, girls," Kendra's mom said.

Kendra frowned and hurried in slippered feet to the phone to call Audrey. No dial tone. *Bummer,* she thought, *the storm's knocked out the phones and it's slowing down our investigation. Wish I had a cell phone.*

She wandered to the window and gazed again at the remains of the blizzard. *I hate the cold weather.* A car crept along in the swath cut by the snowplow. Kendra noticed how very wide the street was. *There's so much space in this town and all the towns wherever we've lived. Lots of room — huge houses on huge lots, and even more on the farms. In the summer, rows and rows of crops as far as the eye can see. And the skies! Skies that go on forever with sunsets too fantastic for words. Shouldn't all this beauty make people notice the good in each other? It doesn't seem to matter. They only care about finding fault, loving any bit of gossip they hear. I can't stand the thought of what they'll say about us when they learn Dad's here and a useless drunk.*

She closed her eyes to wipe away her negative thoughts, and wished for the first sign of spring: the arrival of the sandhill cranes. Every year, thousands of them descended to feed on the dried cornstalks on their way northward. Kendra longed for the day when the huge birds with their distinctive red, white and beige head markings would drop from the sky, bringing spring and warm weather with their magnificent wings.

*****

Monday morning Mom went off to work, but school was cancelled. That left Kendra to watch Toni, who was busily playing with her dollhouse in the bedroom. She wondered if this was how prisoners felt — not able to go anywhere. For the umpteenth time that day, she tried the phone. At last, dial tone!

"Audrey! What a relief. I'm going bonkers here."

Audrey agreed it was no fun being trapped inside for who knew how long. "I haven't been able to get through to Mr. Campbell on my cell, but if your landline's up maybe his is, too."

"I'll try him right now. Why don't you search the Internet for the name of the girl who was molested in Newton? Maybe you'll find a newspaper article or something," Kendra said.

"Deal," said Audrey.

The news from Mr. Campbell left Kendra feeling even lower. He hadn't gotten any leads from Cloud's Aunt Laura, or her neighbor. As if trying to console her, he'd added that his friend was running a background check on Cloud's Uncle Frank.

Kendra called Audrey with the bad news.

"He didn't get anything?" Audrey's voice was incredulous.

"Not a thing," Kendra repeated, unable to hide the disappointment in her voice. "Unbelievable, huh? I'm beginning to see why the police are so slow at solving cases. It's been weeks since Cloud's murder and we keep coming up with nothing."

Kendra hung up and slumped to the floor, mumbling to herself. "Without this case to work on, I've got nothing but a messed-up family and this horrible snow. And we're absolutely nowhere on finding the killer."

Chapter 19

Dammit, he thought, and gave the footstool a vicious kick. *Letting my urges get the best of me.*

He fumed about the day in the dark movie theater. *I know better than to do something that stupid in public.* He paced the tiny living room end-to-end in a few seconds. *But God, that girl with the earmuffs hasn't been back. She's gotta know she's driving me crazy. Driving me to do things — dangerous things.*

Just like Ma. She had to know she couldn't keep on. She had to know there would be a day when I'd grow some and be a man. Being starved and beaten like an animal just wasn't going to happen anymore. Ma forced me to make her stop.

And Pa — I'll bet he's happy he doesn't have to suck up to her ever again. He never did thank me. Bastard!

He stopped pacing and leaned his head on the wall. His shoulders sagged. *I was damned lucky to get out of the theater without getting caught.*

Gotta get myself under control. I just need to wait."Pink earmuffs" will be back.

He tried to ignore the disappointment he felt. But it was impossible. Disappointment changed to frustration and his fist crashed into the wall. *I can't stand it. Need a new plaything! Maybe I should hang out at the mall. They shop in packs, and a stray is bound to break from the herd. Just gotta be careful, that's all.*

Chapter 20

Kendra hunched her slight frame over the computer keyboard in the school library. She had to work fast before the librarian discovered what she was doing. Audrey hadn't been able to come up with the name of the girl who'd been molested at the movie theater in Newton, but Kendra was sure there had to be a way to find her.

First, she searched for a Newton newspaper. No luck. She tried "sexual assaults Nebraska," and got 5,751 items. Kendra's mind numbed. She entered "The Omaha Tribune" – the name of the closest big city newspaper she could remember. Its home page had a link to search back issues. *Yes!* In the topic search box she typed "sexual assaults" with a date range, but when she hit "Enter," a message saying, "Free registration required for stories older than seven days," popped up. The bell rang signaling five minutes until math class. *Darn! No time!*

After school, Kendra told Audrey how she'd gotten close to searching the old archives of the newspaper, but ran out of time. "Let's get online at your place and see if we can find something."

"All right, but I'm sure that newspapers don't print the names of victims in active cases," Audrey said. "But this girl in my social studies class, Emily

Chatterley, has a blog and she's not very smart about what she posts."

"Hmm, I guess her last name fits, huh?" Kendra replied. The girls giggled and raced to Audrey's, excited about their new mission. Side by side, they combed through Emily's blog for what seemed like forever. Shaking her head at the silliness of many of Emily's posts, Kendra said, "This girl needs to get a life."

Just as they were about to give up, the phrase "teenage girl in Newton" caught Kendra's eye. There it was: the girl's name – "Brianna Bennett" – and the name of the development she lived in – "Morningside Heights." No address, but it was a start! Kendra couldn't help grinning, until she realized she didn't know how to find her address or phone number from this little information.

"What are we going to do now?" Kendra demanded of Audrey.

"Have a snack," Audrey replied.

Over Audrey's mom's outrageously delicious peanut butter chocolate chip cookies they blurted out ideas. But they realized almost before they left their lips how lame they were. Then Kendra's eyes lit up. "I know! One of the map websites!"

Audrey gave her a blank stare.

"Come on! I'll show you!" Kendra said. It took a while to find a detailed map of Newton that showed the neighborhoods and the schools, but eventually they pinpointed a Thomas Jefferson Middle School in Morningside Heights. "This has to be it. It's the only middle school in that area."

"Okay. So, how does this get us any closer to finding her phone number?" Audrey asked.

"Just watch." Kendra keyed in the Newton phone directory, and found the middle school's phone number.

"You dummy, the school won't give out her number," Audrey complained. "I may as well start my science homework."

Kendra ignored Audrey's comment, and jotted down the prefix of the school's number. Then she accessed all the Bennetts in the directory. There were three listings, but only one with the same prefix as the school. "This has to be Brianna's house!" Kendra exclaimed.

"Not necessarily. What if she has a stepdad with a different last name?" Audrey challenged. "What if they moved from another area and kept their phone number? What if they have cell phones instead of a landline?"

"So, does that mean we just give up?" Kendra's face flamed. "All right, you do your homework. I'm heading home!"

*****

Peeling off her coat, Kendra rushed to make the call before Mom and Toni came home. Her hand trembled as she dialed the number. It was scary calling a stranger but here she was, doing just that. And on top of it all, she intended to ask this person to talk to her about an unspeakable experience. She started to hang up, but just before her finger touched the button, Kendra heard a faint "Hello?"

Her throat constricted and she swallowed hard to clear it. She stammered, "H-h-hi, this is Kendra Morgan. Is this Brianna Bennett?" Breathlessly she waited for a reply.

There was a long pause. "Yes, this is Brianna."

Oh great, now what? Kendra thought. She remembered hearing somewhere that people will confide in you if you reach out to them first. "I lost my friend to a murderer," she blurted. *What a dumb thing to say,* but she continued to pour out the story in a jumble of sentences, afraid if she stopped, Brianna would hang up.

"That's so horrible!" Brianna exclaimed.

"It is awful, but what I heard happened to you couldn't have been much fun either. I know it must be hard to talk about."

"For sure," Brianna replied, "but now that some time's passed, I'm not so freaked. I can tell you really need help."

"Hey, don't say any more than you want to, okay?"

"Okay," Brianna said. It sounded like she was licking her lips and swallowing. "Well, I didn't get a good look at him. About the only thing I know for sure is that he was tall and thin. He sat down beside me, which seemed strange because the theater wasn't crowded. I thought about going to go find my friend, who was getting a soda, but he started talking about the movie."

"He said something about the chase scene we were watching — he had a nice voice. Usually I don't talk to strangers, but this guy was...I don't know how to describe it — he made me feel it was safe to talk to him. But when he put his hand on my thigh, I was shocked. I couldn't move at first, but I finally pushed him away and ran all the way home without my friend."

"Do you remember what he said?" Kendra could hear the fear in Brianna's voice. It made the hair on her arms stand up.

There was a long pause. "I remember what he asked just before he touched me: 'Do your legs ever rub together when you're watching a movie?' Then he said in a weird voice, 'I'll bet it feels good, huh?' When I think about how his voice cracked, I freeze up inside."

"Oh my God! He really said that?" Kendra gasped. "Do you think you'd recognize his voice if you heard it again?" she asked, willing the sick feeling in the pit of her stomach to vanish.

"I don't know. I was so afraid. But I'd give it a go if it would help find your friend's murderer." Brianna sounded like she'd rather rope and brand a steer with one arm tied behind her back.

"Thanks for talking to me, Brianna. I'm glad you got away from that horrible creep."

"Do you think this guy is the one you're after?" she asked weakly.

"I don't know, but I think it's possible. I'll keep you posted if you like. Bye for now?" Kendra wanted to talk more, but sensed she was close to Brianna's limit.

"Yeah — you take care, Kendra." There was an unmistakable sound of relief in her good-bye.

Returning the phone to its base, Kendra felt something nagging at her. Brianna's description of the man seemed familiar. Suddenly, she knew who it was. *Brent! Tall, lanky, charming Brent Grimsby!* Her heart thudded against her chest as she thought about him. She visualized him swaggering about the bus depot, Maglite swinging at his side; his long, tapered fingers stroking the silver metal of his belt buckle.

Tight bands of pain began to creep from the base of her neck and circle her head. *Another migraine,* she thought. She called Audrey with her suspicions as she wished for the quiet darkness of her bed.

Audrey apologized for not having more faith in her and was excited that Kendra had talked to Brianna. But when Kendra got to her suspicions about Grimsby, Audrey sounded stunned. "Kendra, are you sure? I know what he tried with you was slimy, but some men are pigs. There are a lot of guys matching his description. It's probably just coincidence."

"Brianna said he was easy to talk to — made her feel like he wasn't a stranger at all. That's exactly like Grimsby." She pressed a hand to her forehead. "I've gotta go — another monster headache."

"Okay, we'll talk tomorrow. Why don't you come over and we'll plan our strategy? Plus, we can talk about the Winter Wonderland Dance this weekend. We have to figure out what we're wearing."

"Yeah, okay." Kendra could tell Audrey didn't believe her. "We have to decide what to do about Grimsby, though," she insisted.

"Right, Kendra. Get some rest and I'll call Mr. Campbell and fill him in."

Chapter 21

Kendra woke the next day feeling groggy, but her migraine was gone. As she got Toni ready for daycare, her head began to buzz with thoughts of Brent Grimsby and the case. Then she remembered: the school dance. *What should I wear? I don't have any cute outfits. Will anyone ask me to dance?* Hurrying through the entry doors of the school, she squeezed her eyes shut and willed the school day to vanish. Audrey had a doctor appointment over the lunch hour. That meant waiting through six long classes to meet up with her. It seemed impossible — there was so much to discuss.

Finally, as the last bell sounded, Kendra sprang from her desk. She found Audrey at her locker and they hurried as fast as they could on the icy sidewalks. Dropping their backpacks on the sofa, they ran to her friend's room.

Audrey began pulling clothes from her closet and tossing them on the bed so fast Kendra could scarcely make out their color or style. Her enthusiasm made Kendra temporarily forget about her obsession with finding Cloud's killer.

"What are you waiting for? Start trying them on," Audrey prompted.

While Kendra slipped into a royal blue top and navy skirt, Audrey modeled her new dress with matching jacket. Piling her heavy auburn curls on top of her head, Audrey studied the effect of the green dress with her glowing complexion and hair. "Up or down?" she asked.

"Audrey, you look gorgeous!" Kendra gasped. She couldn't help feeling a twinge of jealousy. Her friend had so much — enough clothes for half the girls at school — and she was pretty besides. It wasn't fair!

Audrey let out a little laugh, as though she was embarrassed at the compliment. Kendra stepped out of the blue outfit and pulled a simple peach dress with a scooped neckline over her head.

"Well, you're pretty hot stuff yourself! Here, I have just the necklace for that dress," Audrey said, fastening a silver choker with coral accents around Kendra's neck. "Wait, I think my crème shawl would be the perfect touch." She grabbed it from the closet and draped it over Kendra's shoulders.

Kendra gazed wide-eyed at the stranger in the mirror, gently stroking the gossamer material of the shawl. She was amazed to find a young woman staring back at her. The jealousy she'd been feeling dissolved into pleasure. She looked every bit as awesome as Audrey.

"It's perfect, Kendra! Don't you love it?"

Kendra only nodded. She didn't speak or move. She knew if she did, the spell would be broken and the image in the mirror would melt away. Audrey came and stood beside her and they each smiled a little smile into the mirror, then big smiles. Finally, they threw their heads back and danced arm in arm around the room until they fell on the bed breathless and giggling.

A fashion frenzy followed. Audrey's cosmetic case, a nail kit with a rainbow of polishes, hair accessories, shoes, and more jewelry soon covered every spare inch of the room. They experimented with eye shadows, eyeliners, mascara, blushes and lip glosses. Then hairstyles: up, down, braided, with and without ribbons, clips and bands. There were so many nail polish colors that Kendra couldn't decide, so she painted each nail a different hue.

At last, they got around to discussing Grimsby.

Sitting at her dressing table, Audrey mumbled around a mouthful of bobby pins. "I called Mr. Campbell to give him your theory about that slimeball being a possible suspect — of course, I didn't tell him you had talked to Brianna in Newton. And I asked him how things were going with his part of the investigation. He said he had asked his ex-cop friend, Jack, to run a background check on Grimsby, as well as Cloud's Uncle Frank."

"Really?" From her perch on Audrey's bed, Kendra's eyebrows went up in surprise.

"He said it seemed suspicious to him, the way Grimsby acted when you went to him for help." She turned from the mirror to face Kendra.

"See, even Mr. Campbell suspects him! Well, what did he find out?" Kendra pulled a pillow close to her chest, as if she could protect herself from Audrey's answer. She was sure there'd be creepy news.

"Nothing. Both men have clean records. Of course, they could be using…what do you call it? Aliases?"

"You're kidding! Nothing?" Kendra exclaimed.

Audrey shrugged.

"I know he's the killer!"

"But we have no proof he was the guy in the movie theater, or that he's done anything wrong," Audrey replied.

"Yeah, we need something definite on him." Kendra released the pillow and stared straight ahead, lost in thought. "Wouldn't it be cool if we had some new technology, like GPS?" Her voice rose with excitement.

"That's how they caught that guy in Kansas who murdered his wife," Audrey said. "The system tracked him driving into the woods to hide some bloodied clothes where he'd already dumped her body. Well, we sure don't have anything that fancy. Let's ask Mr. Campbell if he's got any ideas."

"He won't do anything if Grimsby has a clean record," Kendra said. She concentrated even harder. "I know, we could search his place when we know he's at work. I'm not sure where he lives – I already checked the phone book. Maybe if we shadowed him he'd lead us to his place. It could be really bad if he catches us though." Kendra grabbed the pillow again and clutched it even more tightly than before as she imagined Grimsby's piercing gaze and strong hands reaching out for her. *I must be crazy,* she thought. *Here I am suggesting Audrey and I tail this guy and I'm scared out of my mind.*

She remembered the last time she'd been frightened. It was the day Dad had slowly driven alongside her as she was walking home from school. She had felt hunted. Anger rose up from her belly and burned at her throat. *Why shouldn't I hunt someone for a change? Grimsby is evil! I know he is! He's got to be stopped,* she thought. Kendra turned to face what she knew would be huge objections from Audrey.

Chapter 22

Kendra watched the thousands of circles of light scamper round and round the school gym. They slid over the balloons, crepe paper streamers and dancing couples, careened over the band and cascaded onto the wood floor. She wasn't the only one who wasn't dancing. Most of the kids hung out in groups talking and laughing but Kendra stood alone, mesmerized by the music and the light patterns and the dancers flowing by her. Audrey was dancing with someone named Ben. Kendra didn't remember him from school, but Audrey seemed to like him just fine.

"Would you like to dance?" A voice startled her from her daydream. She turned to find Seth, another friend of Audrey's.

She gulped down her nervousness, and replied, "Sure." Following him onto the floor, they started out by stepping on each other's toes. They laughed and relaxed and fell into the rhythm. By the end of the number, Kendra was having a great time.

A fast tune began and Seth excused himself. *Just when I'm starting to have fun,* Kendra thought. Looking around the room, she spotted Johnny Haskins. Her heart skipped. He was leaning against the gym wall looking bored or lonely — she wasn't sure which. *What the heck*. She skirted the edge of the dance floor, hoping no one would approach him before she got there. The tantalizing beat of the music gave her courage she didn't know she had. Johnny looked up and saw her. A lopsided grin spread over his face.

"Are you gonna ask me to dance?" he asked.

"Thought I might," she said, trying to hide her nervousness.

"Okay. I guess that's what we're here for, huh?" He tentatively reached for her hand. Kendra laced her fingers in his as they danced their way onto the floor. Audrey and Ben spotted them and bounced over to say hello. Kendra marveled at how much fun dancing was, and when the tune ended and a slow dance began, Johnny pulled her to him.

As they danced together, Kendra felt like one of the magic circles of light spinning weightlessly through the night. She couldn't remember when she'd been this happy.

Chapter 23

Kendra spent New Year's Eve watching videos and eating popcorn with Toni. Mom had asked her to babysit so she could go to a party with Dad. Knowing there was nothing she could do about who Mom spent her time with, she had reluctantly agreed. *Audrey's babysitting her cousins, so I guess it won't kill me,* she thought.

The movie "The Iron Giant" was about a huge creature that fed on metal. "Look Kendra, he's eating the railroad track," cried Toni, "And there's a train coming!" Her enthusiasm was so contagious, Kendra almost found herself getting into the little kids' story. But she kept thinking how glad she was the holidays were nearly done. The dance had been the most fun ever, but the rest of the holiday celebrations got in the way of working on the case.

After several attempts to convince Audrey to dig into Grimsby's life, her friend had finally agreed. "But if I do this, you have to promise a double date with Ben and Johnny."

Kendra had said yes even though she knew she didn't have the nerve to ask Johnny out. *I'm going to find the killer, no matter what,* she'd thought.

Since Grimsby wasn't listed in the Finchville phone book, they'd searched the Internet. That had come up empty. Well, not exactly empty. One Brent Grimsby had surfaced, but after digging into his history, it turned out he was 92 years old. That had given them a good laugh.

"Our only chance is to follow him from the bus depot and hope he goes home for lunch," Kendra had said. "I remember the day when I ran to tell him about seeing Billy Ray with Cloud's hair clip. I still trusted him then. It was about four o'clock, and that's where he was headed."

"How is finding out where he lives going to help us?" Audrey had asked.

Kendra shrugged. "I don't know. Maybe we'll learn something about him from his neighbors."

"You don't think they'll tell him we're snooping around?" Audrey had arched an eyebrow at her friend.

"Don't get yourself all worked up. I'm just thinking out loud. Let's just see if we can find out where he lives, and we'll plan our next step after that."

"Oh, all right!" Audrey had grudgingly agreed.

Whenever they could get away without Audrey's parents getting suspicious, they'd head to the depot, hoping to catch their suspect leaving. Days went by without a glimpse of him. Either he was eating lunch in the depot or he was getting past them somehow.

"Oh no, the train's going to run over the giant," exclaimed Toni, breaking into Kendra's thoughts. She wiggled closer to Kendra.

"Wow, looks like he's really in trouble now." Kendra tried to sound excited.

They finished watching the video, climbed into their warmest pajamas, brushed their teeth and padded into the bedroom where Toni slept on a small trundle bed at the foot of Mom's bed. "Happy New Year, little one," Kendra said, tucking the covers around her.

Toni rubbed her eyes. "I'm not tired. Can I watch the giant again?"

"If you do, you'll be on your own 'cuz I'm going to bed." Kendra smiled at the sight of Toni's eyelids fluttering.

"'Tomorrow?" she said through a yawn.

"Yeah, tomorrow." Kendra bent to hug her. *She's such a little sweetie sometimes,* she thought.

"I lub you Kendra," Toni said, wrapping her arms tightly around her sister's neck.

"I love you, too. Now go to sleep." Kendra planted a big kiss on her sister's chubby cheek, then settled Toni's teddy bear in the crook of her arm and patted her through the covers. *It hasn't been such a bad evening after all,* she thought.

*****

Kendra slept fitfully, dreaming disjointedly of Brent Grimsby. In one, he was his usual charming self and she felt no fear of him. In another, he crept through their apartment. Cowering in the locked bathroom, she heard him systematically search each room. Certain she was going to die she opened her mouth to scream, but no sound escaped. Toni's face floated before her – she wanted to hug her and never let go.

She woke with a start, too terrified to move. Peering into the darkness, Kendra saw the familiar shape of her backpack hanging from a chair. She told herself it was just a nightmare, but she couldn't shake the horrible feeling of doom.

Once, a long time ago, Kendra had fallen asleep in the car waiting for Dad to come out of the Red Dog Bar. She had waited with Mom and Toni for what seemed forever in the cold January night. Finally, Mom had turned off the engine and disappeared under the neon light. As the minutes ticked by, Kendra had pulled the tattered blanket under her chin, and snuggled closer to Toni. She must've fallen asleep with her mouth open, because when she woke her jaw was so stiff with cold she couldn't close it. As she had worked away the ache, she realized that it would be the same when she died. Not only her mouth — but her eye sockets, nose and ears, too. And her insides: heart, lungs, liver, guts — all cold and still. Cloud Nicholson was laying in her grave like that, her body stiff and blue-cold in death.

Was she being foolish, thinking she and Audrey could catch Cloud's murderer without becoming another of his victims? It had crossed her mind more than once, but the stark reality of the possible consequences hadn't really sunk in until now. She thought about it for a long time and finally went to the kitchen for hot chocolate to shake her gloomy mood. Gray morning light was beginning to filter into the room before Kendra crawled beneath the covers and fell asleep again.

*****

Bustling about the kitchen, Ivan Campbell put the last dish in the cupboard. He glanced worriedly about, realizing he wasn't the best judge of whether everything looked presentable. Laura Nicholson obviously had higher standards than his when it came to housekeeping. He recalled how her kitchen had sparkled.

"Damn," Ivan muttered, eyeing the spider web in the corner of the window over the sink. He'd intentionally left the little spider to its devices, not having the heart to destroy its home. But now he gingerly lifted as much of the web as he could with its owner and some unlucky fly corpses. Carrying it to the porch, he placed it on a large Christmas cactus. *Glad I got this porch covered for the winter,* he thought as he hurried back into the kitchen, grabbed the Windex and paper towels, and cleaned the window. *If Laura thinks I'm a slob, I may be a goner.* A knock interrupted his regrets.

"Here I am as promised, ready to meet the family," Laura announced cheerfully. "Good to get out on New Year's Day. So often we're snowed in." She smiled as she removed her gloves.

Ivan smiled in return and felt his apprehension melt into something more like bliss. He hadn't felt this way for so long, he wasn't sure what it was, but he liked it.

"Come in, Laura. Yes, it's very good to have clear roads, and better yet to see you." He tried not to sound as excited as he was. A soft, floral scent floated into the room with her. Taking her coat, he steered her by the elbow to the living room where Bubba and Mandy slept. "I'm sorry, but Kendra and Audrey won't be here. I've tried to call, but haven't connected with them."

"Oh, they're gorgeous! Just as you described them." Laura threw up her hands and went over to Bubba. "I remember you said that Mandy's a bit shy so I'll talk to Bubba first." Sitting on the sofa beside the huge cat, she stroked him and struck up a conversation as if he were a friend of many years. Bubba responded with a languid stretch and a look that seemed to say, "You woke me up, but I forgive you because you're a human and don't know any better."

Ivan beamed as he settled on the ottoman. "You're right to do that. Mandy will be over when she can't stand Bubba getting all the attention."

It was hard to say who enjoyed the getting-to-know-the-cats process the most, but everyone was happy when Ivan and Laura moved on to look at the doll collection. She was amazed at the huge display and Ivan suggested she take one home.

"Oh, I couldn't! I'm sure they're valuable as collectors' items and, more than that, very special to you," Laura said, as she straightened the ruffled apron over a checked gingham dress on a porcelain doll.

Clearing his throat, Ivan said, "Well, you're turning out to be pretty special to me, too. I hope I'm not being too forward, but I'd love it if you'd go to supper with me. Freddy's Fire Pit has great barbecue." He held his breath and waited for her reply.

"Sounds wonderful, but only on the condition I can return the favor — maybe a home-cooked meal at my place next time." Laura put her hand on his shoulder and smiled into his eyes.

A bit later they waited for their supper in a cozy booth at the restaurant. Ivan apologized again for Kendra and Audrey's absence. "I kind of worry about those two," he said.

"Why?" She cocked her head in interest.

"I don't know if they fully realize the trouble they might get into." He slathered butter on a giant slab of corn bread. "Young people think they can do anything. It's been that way forever."

"Ah," Laura replied.

Ivan added, "I don't think their parents know what they're doing. There is a woman who's a friend of Kendra's. Her name's Peg Strong. I suspect she knows what they've been up to. That's the only reason I haven't said anything to their parents yet." Ivan realized at that instant he needed someone like Laura to talk to, especially about Kendra and Audrey. He was beginning to feel more than a little responsible for the two adventurers.

"Good," Laura said. "Maybe you could get in touch with Peg and compare notes. I don't know what else you can do, other than keep in close contact with the girls. If you call their parents, they'll cut you off for sure."

"Yeah, and they're so determined — especially Kendra. I don't think even their parents could stop them. They trust me and I think they're keeping me in the loop so far."

"Best to keep on with what you're doing then. And ask lots of questions!" Laura pointed her fork at him and then dug into her salad.

"Yes, ma'am! I like no-nonsense women like you!" Ivan said.

"And I haven't met a man like you in forever!" Laura tipped her glass to him.

Chapter 24

The next week arrived crisp and cold. Kendra could hardly wait for the school day to end so they could follow their suspect. And yet she was afraid of what might happen. The nightmare on New Year's Eve had made her realize how scared she really was, yet she felt more determined than ever to find the maniac who had killed her friend. She needed to talk to Audrey. For some reason, she could think about a problem for hours and not come up with a solution. But when she said it out loud, it switched her brain to the "on" position.

At lunch, they sat alone in a corner of the cafeteria. Kendra told Audrey about her nightmare. The smell of greasy fries made her stomach lurch. "It made me think, like, what if this creep realizes we're stalking him and comes after us?"

"Geez, Kendra!" Audrey scowled. "I've been trying to put those ideas out of my head."

"Yeah, but what if?"

"I told you, I don't want to think about it!" Audrey exclaimed, her eyes wide as a jackrabbit's.

"Neither do I." Suddenly, Kendra's brain found the "on" button.

"I know! We should write a letter to our folks and leave it where they'll find it if we disappear.

Even if it's too late for us, they'll know who to go after. I could leave it with my notes on the case. That way Mom will have the whole picture." Kendra looked at Audrey for her reaction. "And we can't tell Mr. Campbell any of this, okay?"

"I don't like it, Kendra. This is getting too wild for me." Audrey grabbed her lunch tray and hurried away before Kendra could utter another word.

*****

A couple of days had passed and Kendra hoped Audrey had calmed down. "How about we head over to the bus depot after school today?" Kendra asked.

"I don't think so," Audrey replied, "your little talk about writing 'goodbye' letters made me see how stupid we're being."

"Come on, we'll be super careful. We haven't been caught yet, have we?"

"Nope, and I don't plan to be!" Audrey's eyes flashed.

Kendra drew her trump card. "I'm going alone then." Her mouth was set in a firm line.

"Aw, Kendra. You can't do that," Audrey whined.

"Come on, then!"

A short time later, the girl sleuths were stationed across the street from the depot, using the trunk of a huge elm tree for cover. Kendra was so busy trying to coax Audrey out of her sulk, she almost missed seeing their suspect stride through the door. "There he is! Give him a head start, and then we'll cross the street and follow," Kendra whispered excitedly.

He took such long steps he was nearly out of sight before they knew it. "Come on, we're going to have to hustle to keep up." Kendra grabbed Audrey's arm and pulled her along.

They didn't have to worry about discovery. Their mark seemed focused on a mission and never once looked back. Several blocks from the bus depot, he turned up a sidewalk to a large brick apartment building.

"Hurry up, we've got to see which unit he goes into," Kendra huffed.

He stopped to check his mail at a row of mailboxes in front of The Hearthstone Apartments. They caught up in time to see him disappear into Unit #8.

"Enough already. Let's get out of here," Audrey said breathlessly as they crouched behind a row of shrubbery.

"Wait. Let's hide out until he leaves. Then we can snoop around a bit," Kendra urged her friend.

"Are you kidding? Let's get out of here!" Audrey demanded.

"But you agreed to come," Kendra protested, her voice rising to match Audrey's.

"I know, but I'm scared. He looks really slimy to me. I don't know, maybe it's his slithery walk — but whatever it is, I don't want to see him again!" Audrey glared at her friend.

A part of Kendra wanted to run, too, but somehow she had to convince them both to stay. Pushing away the anxiety that threatened to sneak into her voice, she said, "This might be our only chance to get something on him. We won't be in any danger. He has to go back to work until midnight. We'll be long gone by then."

Audrey's shoulders slumped. "Oh, all right – but you have to promise you'll leave when I say!"

"No problem. I'm with you." Kendra sighed with relief and steered Audrey toward a convenience store across the street where they could wait.

Twenty interminable minutes passed before their suspect appeared and headed down the block. The girls emerged from their observation post behind the magazine rack where they'd pretended to be interested in the latest issue of Teen magazine.

Darkness was falling and there seemed to be little movement around the apartments. "Most people are still at work," Kendra murmured. "That's lucky for us. Come on, let's look around back." Following the sidewalk around the building, they discovered a courtyard with back doors to each apartment. Unit #8 was the second from the end.

"Maybe our luck will include a key under his mat." Kendra lifted a tattered rug to find nothing but a sprinkling of rock salt. As her eyes adjusted to the dim light, she noticed a flower box on the windowsill with frozen flower stalks standing like soldiers in a row. There was a small space between the bottom of the flower box and the windowsill. Leaning over the porch rail, she ran her fingers slowly along the space. "Here it is!" she exclaimed, holding the key up to Audrey. "Give it a try." She was shaking so hard she was sure she couldn't maneuver the key.

Audrey cringed. "No way! You're crazy!"

It took Kendra several tries before the key turned in the lock. She got behind Audrey and pushed her into what appeared to be a kitchenette. Closing the door behind them, Kendra peered into the darkness. She pulled a small LED flashlight from her pocket.

Dirty dishes and overflowing ashtrays were piled on the kitchen counters. There was nothing on the walls, except a plaque with a poem that read something about beer being bachelor's milk.

"Kendra, this is breaking and entering!" Audrey hissed. "I didn't want to bust into Mr. Campbell's place and now you've got me doing it again!"

Kendra headed down a short hallway in the semi-darkness, stumbling over shoes and clothes thrown here and there. "You wouldn't leave me here alone, would you?" Kendra challenged.

"Dammit, Kendra!" Audrey muttered as she followed her friend to the bedroom. More clothes littered the unmade bed, a chair, and the floor.

"Look under the pillows," Kendra commanded. "Then lift up the end of the mattress so I can look underneath." Her plan was to stay busy so they wouldn't think about being afraid.

"Yes, ma'am!" Audrey replied, the anger in her voice unmistakable as she threw the pillows to the floor. Looking in the bed and under the mattress revealed nothing.

Kendra fell to her knees to look beneath the bed. Recoiling at the sight of a revolver in a leather holster resting snugly next to the bed frame, she jumped up and hurried to the closet with Audrey close behind.

Kendra pushed the thought of the gun from her mind in an effort to stay calm. Several cardboard boxes sat beneath the clothes which hung eerily like emaciated scarecrows. *Oh no, it's getting worse,* Kendra thought as she shone the flashlight on the cover of a magazine. It showed a nude woman in a provocative pose.

"That's totally disgusting!" Audrey stammered as she looked over Kendra's shoulder.

Scattered amongst the magazines were photographs. Kendra's hand trembled as she held them up to the flashlight's beam. *I wonder if he took these?* "What a pervert!" Kendra said. She was stunned as her eyes made out scantily dressed bodies doing unspeakable things. The subjects were mostly girls and very young women, all looking unhappy. Even those who smiled had sad, vacant looks. It made her feel sad, too. *How had they come to be in such awful circumstances?*

Then Kendra noticed a box with something fuzzy sticking out. *A stuffed animal? No, it was a pair of hot pink earmuffs.* She felt Audrey looking over her shoulder. Underneath, they could see other female items — mostly underwear. Kendra couldn't help but wonder if any of them belonged to Cloud.

"I don't feel so good," Audrey muttered. "Let's go."

Kendra knew Audrey was at her limit and she felt queasy, too. She took a deep breath to steady herself. Then Kendra heard a door opening. She put her finger to her lips and pulled Audrey into the back of the closet and switched off the flashlight.

Someone was talking! Who was it? Soon Kendra realized it was Grimsby talking to himself. Over the thudding of her heart, she made out snippets of conversation: "...Damn fool — home for lunch, forget to eat — busy daydreaming of foxy little bitches — better take some cigs, too." Sounds of the refrigerator door closing and the whir of a can opener were followed by the closing of an outside door and fading footsteps.

It was several minutes before the girls could move or speak.

"I think he's gone," Kendra whispered.

"Are you sure?" Audrey spoke through clenched teeth.

Kendra switched her flashlight on to see Audrey's enormous eyes staring into her own.

Then Audrey's face contorted and she put her head down on her knees and sobbed huge racking sobs that shook her whole body.

Kendra could only put her arm around her friend and hold her, all the while feeling guilty for putting her best friend through this hell.

After several minutes, Audrey's sobs turned to hiccups. Finally, she swiped at her eyes and said, "Let's go."

Shakily, they made their way out of the apartment. Peeking out the door for any signs of movement, they found it still and dark, so they slipped the key back into its hiding place. As soon as they were away from the building, they grabbed hands and ran as fast as they could for home. When they reached the place where they went to their own homes, they hugged each other hard.

"I'm so glad we got out of there without getting caught," Audrey said. "This detective stuff isn't the fun I thought it would be. No more, Kendra. Can't do it anymore! "

"I'm with you," Kendra replied. "Call me the second you get home, okay?" Hurrying down the darkened street, her mind spun with what they'd discovered. Grimsby certainly looked guilty. *But Audrey would never be persuaded to stay with the case now.* She would never forget the fear she'd seen in her friend's eyes. And as she considered how close they'd been to being discovered, she questioned her own courage, too.

Chapter 25

The next day at lunch, Kendra glanced around to be sure no one was listening in on their conversation. She laughed inwardly to herself. *Fat chance with the noise decibels in here,* she thought. "I wish we'd taken some of the girls' clothing from Grimsby's place. Mr. Campbell might have been able to get his cop friend to check it for DNA."

Kendra sighed. "But if we call the cops now and tell them we broke in, it'll just get us in trouble. And if by some miracle they do listen to us, and it turns out there's some other explanation for that stuff being there, we'll really be in a mess. Gosh, with all the dirty stuff in the movies and on TV, those photos might not raise any suspicions at all."

Audrey glared at her.

Kendra plunged ahead. "So what do we do now? Should we follow the creep on his day off? I think I could get Mom to tell me when he's not working without making her suspicious."

Kendra tried to keep her voice light as she watched Audrey's face for a reaction. "We'd be very careful not to let him see us, and if we're lucky, we might get some super-good evidence." She failed in her attempt to sound nonchalant when she thought about what Grimsby might be up to next. "We've got to do something — he could be stalking another girl!"

Audrey's gaze flew from her cupcake wrapper to Kendra's face. She muttered, "You go right ahead, Kendra Morgan, but I'm done with this stuff! I already told you that, and you agreed! We need to tell Mr. Campbell or Peg what we know and let them take it from here!"

"But Audrey, we're so close! We just need a little more evidence and the cops will be all over him!" In the next breath she was reminding herself to calm down and give Audrey a little time to think. She took a spoonful of kiwi strawberry yogurt and said softly, "Let's just think about it for a day or two. There's got to be some way to get more on this guy and still stay safe."

"I'm not going anywhere near him or his apartment, and that's final!"

Throughout her afternoon classes, Kendra puzzled over what to do. Without Audrey's help, she felt her resolve fading. If only she knew Johnny Haskins better; maybe he'd be willing to help. When they'd talk before English class, he made her feel like she was the only one in the universe. Somehow she knew he'd protect her no matter what.

She was lost in thought when old Mrs. Hathamore — better known as Mrs. Dinosaur by her students — called on Kendra to tell the class where Abraham Lincoln was the night he was shot.

Stammering a little, Kendra replied, "At a parade in Dallas, Texas."

"Miss Morgan, you not only have your presidents confused, but your centuries as well!"

Mrs. Hathamore frowned. "See me after class, young lady."

Oh great, Kendra thought, *now I've got her to deal with! Guess it serves me right. I've been letting this case take over my life.* She felt the muscles at the back of her neck begin to tighten into hard knots and knew another migraine was on the way.

As soon as she met with her teacher and grudgingly accepted the extra homework assignment as punishment for her stupidity in class, Kendra rushed home, threw her books on her bed, and swallowed two Excedrin. She refused to give in to the headache from hell until she had a plan. *I know! My notes. Maybe I'm overlooking something really obvious.*

Settling herself on the lumpy sofa, she began reading from the beginning. As she read, she thought about the people they'd suspected and ruled out: Billy Ray, Mr. Campbell, and Cloud's Uncle Frank.

She remembered how disappointed she and Audrey had been when Mr. Campbell told them that Frank had an airtight alibi. Mr. Campbell's ex-cop friend had discovered that after dropping Cloud off, Frank had gone to another party. Several people there had vouched for him.

Kendra didn't look up until she finished with the last entry dated the day before: "Tuesday, January 4th: Searched Grimsby's apartment. Discovered gun, porno magazines, disgusting photos and a box of girls' items. Plus heard him talk to himself about young girls!"

Little rocks of disappointment settled in her stomach. Nothing had jumped out at her from the lined pages. She knew in her heart that Grimsby was guilty. *But how was she going to prove it? Was this how it would end? So close, and yet a million miles away?* Her head and neck screamed with pain. Pulling a frayed quilt from the back of the sofa, she curled up on her side and closed her eyes.

The next night, Kendra picked up her notes again. *There had to be a clue she was missing. There just had to be!* She began reading again. On the very first page, her eyes fell on a name: Billy Ray. *Maybe he could help. After all, wasn't he the one who'd found Cloud's barrette right after her murder?*

She called Audrey from her bedroom so Mom wouldn't hear. "Let's talk to him! I don't know why we didn't think of it sooner. He may know something even if he isn't so smart." Kendra held her breath, waiting for Audrey's answer.

Audrey sighed. "You just never give up, do you?"

"Pretty please?"

"Oh, all right! At least it's not dealing with you-know-who! I'll have no more to do with that slimeball!"

"Thank you, thank you, thank you, Audrey! I heard Billy Ray was afraid of the police. I'll bet he didn't tell them everything."

Kendra's pleasure at hearing Audrey's response was short-lived when she realized the stupidity of what she'd suggested. Horrified, she blurted out, "What if Billy Ray knows I'm the one who turned him in? He looks like one of those sumo wrestler guys, Audrey."

"Maybe he knows you turned him in, maybe he doesn't. We're just going to have to risk it. Dammit, Kendra, you're the one pulling me back into this. Talking to Billy Ray is a great idea! That's why I said I'd do it," Audrey sputtered.

For an instant Kendra considered asking Audrey to go without her, but didn't dare to risk her friend changing her mind. Plus, she realized her need to know what was happening was stronger than her fear of Billy Ray. "Okay, okay. So when do we go?"

"Tomorrow after school," Audrey said with uncharacteristic firmness.

*****

The next day as they walked to Billy Ray's house, Audrey asked Kendra if she'd written the letter to her mom in case anything happened to them.

"Yeah, did you?" Kendra wanted Audrey to talk first. In fact, she didn't want to think about it right now. It was a yucky subject; plus, at the moment she was fixated on how Billy Ray would react to her. *If he knew she was the one who reported him to the police, would he freak?* She'd seen how strong her dad was, and Billy Ray was twice his size.

"No way. It would force me to think that I could be the second dead fourteen-year-old in Finchville. And thinking about never seeing my family again is just too scary," Audrey added.

"I know what you mean. I wouldn't miss my dad, but Mom and Toni — well, that would be terrible." Kendra tried to fight off the feeling of dread that surrounded her more and more lately.

"So is your dad still around?" Audrey asked.

Kendra heaved a deep sigh. "Boy, you're really on the happy topics today, aren't you?" She gave Audrey a stern look. "Well, if you've gotta know, he's still on his sober streak. And as usual, Mom's getting her hopes up." All the tension Kendra had been feeling over the last few days spilled out. "It makes me so mad! How can she be such an idiot?"

"Maybe she still loves him. Maybe she wants you and Toni to have a dad."

Kendra shook her head stubbornly. How could Audrey understand in her cotton candy world? "Let's talk about something else," she demanded, actually relieved that Billy Ray's house was just around the corner.

"Right," Audrey answered. They walked a little while in silence. "Isn't that the house there?" She pointed to a gray rambler with a turquoise door.

As they approached, they saw a woman washing the last of a Christmas scene from the inside of a picture window. Seeing the girls come up the walk, she answered the door with a curious expression. "Can I help you?"

"Yes, um, are you Mrs. Houston, Billy Ray's mom?" Kendra asked. Her mouth felt parched.

"That's right. Do you know him?" Mrs. Houston looked carefully at the girls as they spoke. "I know all of Billy Ray's friends and I don't remember you."

"I go to the same church and I've seen you and your family there," Kendra answered, trying to stay cool under her hard stare.

She held the door open for them to enter. "Oh, I do remember you now; you attend by yourself. But what do you want with my son?"

The girls stepped into the hallway.

"We have a huge favor to ask, Mrs. Houston." There was a long pause while Kendra searched for words. "The girl that was killed a few months ago — Cloud Nicholson — she was a friend of ours. We're helping some grownups try to solve her murder, and we think Billy Ray may know something more.

If we could just talk to him, we promise we won't do anything to scare him." Kendra forced herself to look into Mrs. Houston's searching eyes.

Mrs. Houston looked down at the cleaning rag in her hands, then at both of the girls. "You know Billy Ray's not as...m-mmm...as advanced as you are. In fact, he's pretty much like a child in a man's body. It's easy to frighten or confuse him. He was a mess after spending a night in jail. I don't want him to go through that upset again. Do you understand me?" The tone of her voice left no room for an ounce of misunderstanding.

Both girls nodded their heads vigorously and Audrey spoke for the first time. "Don't worry, Mrs. Houston. You can trust us. We won't do or say anything to make him afraid."

Mrs. Houston sighed with resignation. "All right, then. You'll find him at Carlisle Park. He likes watching the squirrels and birds there. But mind you, I'll be along in a little while to see he's okay." She opened the door quickly for them to go as though she might change her mind if she delayed another second.

"Thank you, Mrs. Houston. We knew you'd want to do what you can to help find Cloud's killer. You won't be sorry; we promise," Kendra reassured her as she silently thanked the heavens for Audrey. She could never have done this alone.

*****

At the park, the girls found Billy Ray crouched beneath the tall cottonwood trees clapping his gloved hands together. He hunched forward to protect himself from the chill of the January wind.

"Hi, Billy Ray," Kendra called.

"Who are you?" he asked, standing as the girls approached.

"I'm Kendra and this is Audrey. I go to your church. Your mother said it was okay for us to talk to you."

"She did?"

Kendra relaxed a little when no look of recognition appeared on his face — only bewilderment. *Maybe he doesn't know I'm the one who turned him in, or maybe he's forgotten,* she thought. *Next step: get him to trust us.* Kendra pointed to some biscuits tossed on the ground a few yards away. "What's that?"

"Treats for my critters."

"Hmm. You like to feed them?" Kendra asked.

Billy Ray smiled and motioned them to a nearby bench. "Yeah, come and sit down. You might see one-a the little fellas."

"Thanks, Billy Ray. We'd like to, wouldn't we, Audrey?" Kendra motioned Audrey to the bench with her.

"Sure. It's great you're taking care of the little guys," Audrey replied. They settled themselves on the bench next to this giant of a man.

"In the wintertime, they're real hungry. They show up pretty quick, but we gotta be real quiet."

After a few minutes with no creatures in sight, Audrey nudged Kendra with her elbow and whispered in her ear. "I'm freezing. Get on with it."

Well, here goes nothing, Kendra thought as she turned to Billy Ray. "Could we ask you something? We'll talk softly so we don't scare the animals away."

"Okay," Billy Ray replied.

Choosing her words carefully, Kendra said, "We're trying to find the man who hurt our friend, Cloud. We heard you found something of hers and turned it into the police."

There was such a long silence that Kendra wondered if he remembered what she was talking about.

"You mean that hair thingy?"

"Yeah," Kendra replied.

Billy Ray jumped up. "Am I in trouble? Do I gotta go to the police station again?"

"No, you're not in any trouble. We just want to find the person who hurt our friend. You might be the only one who can help us," Kendra said. She looked intently up into his round eyes.

"You could be a hero, Billy Ray," Audrey interjected. "Like Batman or Superman."

"A hero?" Billy Ray straightened.

"Is there anything you remember besides the hair clip?" Kendra pressed.

"Batman? I could really be like Batman?" His round eyes were rounder than ever.

"Sure," Kendra agreed.

His face scrunched in concentration. Then he brightened. "There was somethin'! The shiny, black shoes with 'lil sparkly stones. Like the stones on the hair thingy. I knew my critters would love 'em. When the sun comes round in the spring, they're gonna be so happy!" A grin spread across his face.

"What do you mean, Billy Ray?" Kendra's heart leapt.

"When they see the purdy stones shining in the sun they'll wanna keep 'em," he explained. "Then there'll be a contest to see who gets them and hides them first!" He chuckled to himself.

"Billy Ray, do you know where the shoes are now?" Kendra tried to control the excitement in her voice.

"Yup. I got 'em hid." He rose and lumbered toward the ball field, with the girls at his heels. At an equipment shed bordering the baseball diamond, they watched as he retrieved a plastic bag from a small opening beneath the shed. Through the dirty plastic, they saw a pair of black patent leather pumps with a low heel. A cluster of rhinestones in a daisy pattern across the top was barely visible.

"Billy Ray, this is terrific! Could we borrow them for awhile? They'll definitely help us find our friend's killer!" Kendra said.

"But I never got the hair thingy back," he protested. He clutched the bag to his chest and rocked back and forth.

Kendra and Audrey exchanged worried glances. "I promise we're just borrowing them for a little while, 'kay?" Kendra pleaded. She wanted to soothe him somehow, but didn't know what to do. Then putting her fear aside, she stepped close and patted him on the back. "You'll have them back before you know it. And you'll be a hero, just like Batman."

The girls waited breathlessly.

After a bit, he stopped swaying and looked forlornly at the shoes. "It's the right thing to do, isn't it? Mama always says 'Billy Ray, you'll never be sorry if you do the right thing.'"

"Your mama will be so proud of you!" Kendra nodded and smiled.

He squared his shoulders and handed the shoes to her. "I gotta get back to my critters."

"We'll go with you," Kendra said as the trio headed back to the bench. "I'm sure they'll be here soon. Then we'll walk you home and you can tell your mama what a great thing you did."

Settled once again on the cold bench, it wasn't long before a gray squirrel scampered within a few feet of where they sat. Curling his nimble paws around a morsel of biscuit, he busily gobbled the treat. Kendra and Audrey couldn't help laughing in delight at the way his whiskers shot up and down as he enjoyed his meal. As they watched, more squirrels came for the feast and a huge crow flapped in from nowhere and landed directly at Billy Ray's feet.

"Gwen, where you been?" he said as he held a piece of biscuit out to the purple-black bird, which hopped about sizing up the strangers. "It's okay. They won't hurt you." Gwen took the food and then sprang to Billy Ray's outstretched hand, and from there to his meaty shoulder.

The girls gasped in surprise.

"How'd you get her to do that?" Kendra asked.

"Took a long time, but she knows I'm her friend now." The crow bent her head towards Billy Ray's neck and made a rapid clicking sound.

Somehow it reminded Kendra of the purring of a cat. She wouldn't have been surprised if the crow curled up for a nap on his big, protective shoulder.

Billy Ray beamed and stroked the bird with his gloved hand.

Kendra was glad they'd stayed with Billy Ray even though she could hardly wait to deliver Cloud's shoes to the police. A twinge of guilt stabbed at her for the way she had thought of him in the past: *someone not smart enough to work the microwave. Boy was I wrong. He knows a lot about animals and people. And he cares about all of them. I know some really smart people who could take some lessons from Billy Ray. He lives in his heart and that's a big place to live.*

She and Audrey walked Billy Ray home. They hid their impatience to be on their way while he proudly showed his mama the shoes and told her how he was giving them up to help Cloud. Saying their goodbyes to Billy Ray and Mrs. Houston, they hurried down the porch steps.

"I can't believe I was ever afraid of him! He's a sweetheart!" Kendra exclaimed.

"Come on!" Audrey exclaimed, as she bolted in the direction of the police station.

Chapter 26

As they rushed to the police station, Kendra nudged Audrey. "Call Mr. Campbell and tell him we have Cloud's shoes," she murmured.

Audrey pulled her cell phone from her pocket. No answer. She left him a nearly unintelligible message about their find.

"He'll be so happy!" Kendra said. "I can't wait to tell him in person."

Breathlessly, Kendra and Audrey presented themselves at the front desk of the Finchville Police Station.

An officer swiveled in his chair to see a pair of wide-eyed girls. "Can I help you?"

"We need to speak to the person in charge of the Cloud Nicholson investigation." Kendra stammered.

"Oh. Why's that?" He sauntered up to the counter.

Could he possibly move any slower? Kendra thought. "We have new evidence."

"That so? Well, the detective in charge is out, but you can fill out this form and I'll take care of it." He slapped a piece of paper onto the counter and reached for the shoes.

Kendra stepped back, hugging the package. She heard the indifference in his voice. *He's not taking us seriously,* she thought. "No. Get us someone who's working on the case," she said firmly.

Audrey looked at Kendra in disbelief.

The officer hitched up his pants. He clenched his jaw. "Impertinent little twerp, aren't you?"

Kendra barged ahead. "If there isn't anyone here now, we'll come back later." She turned toward the door.

"Hold up there — let me see if there's anyone else around." He shook his head and stomped away.

"Kendra, I can't believe you were so mouthy with him!" Audrey exclaimed.

"He thinks we're just a couple of dumb kids. I don't trust him to get the shoes to the right person." Secretly, Kendra was amazed at her nerve. *It wasn't long ago I couldn't force myself to even enter a police station. Now I'm talking back to a cop!*

The girls settled themselves in steel-rimmed upholstered chairs to wait. The officer returned and muttered, "The detective just came in." Kendra tried not to smile.

A few minutes passed before a woman approached. "Hi, I'm Detective Goodwin." She glanced at the package Kendra clutched as she shook hands with them and explained she was the head of the team investigating the Nicholson murder. "I understand you've got some evidence for us."

"Yes, we've got Cloud's shoes," Kendra said.

The investigator raised her eyebrows. "Let's go back to my desk and we'll fill out a report." She was nearly as wide as she was tall, but she walked with authority.

The girls were all eyes as they followed the detective into a big room with several desks. This was where crimes were solved and bad people brought down.

"Have a seat, girls." The woman pulled over another chair from an adjoining desk for Audrey.

It turned out the detective was very thorough. She asked lots of questions about Kendra and Audrey before she ever got to the topic of Cloud. Then she requested they start at the beginning about how they got involved in the case.

The girls told her how they'd met Mr. Campbell through their landscaping business.

"We persuaded him to help on the case," Kendra continued. She was careful to omit the fact that they had originally searched his house because they had once considered him a suspect.

Kendra and Audrey went through all their sleuthing activities, leaving out their surveillance of Brent Grimsby and their eventual breaking and entering of his apartment. But they did tell her about the time he had hit on Kendra.

"Mr. Campbell thinks he should definitely be considered a person of interest," Kendra said.

The detective looked up from her notes when she heard Kendra say the words, "person of interest." "You're really into this, aren't you?"

Kendra nodded. She could scarcely believe that the Detective Goodwin seemed to take everything they told her seriously. An hour later, they flounced past the dismissive officer at the front desk.

Out on the street, Audrey asked, "Can you believe it?"

"I know! It's incredible! But she said she'd follow up. I think she will, too," Kendra replied.

Audrey heaved a huge sigh. "Now we can leave this whole mess to the police. Let's stop by Mickey D's to celebrate."

Intent on discussing their relief that the investigation was over for them, the girls didn't notice Johnny Haskins until he slid into the booth next to Kendra. "Whatcha talking about?"

Kendra felt Johnny's leg against hers and her pulse quickened.

Audrey shoved her French fries at him. "Oh, nothing."

"Didn't sound like nothin' to me," Johnny said. "Something about the cops and Cloud's shoes? Sounds wild."

Kendra gave Audrey a look. "I think it's okay to tell him. Our part's done now." *What am I saying?* she thought.

"Come on, give it up," Johnny pressed.

Kendra realized she was powerless in the wake of Johnny's charm. "Dude, you have to promise not to tell anyone. We could get in real trouble," she said.

"What kind of trouble?"

"The kind that grounds us 'til high school graduation," Audrey said. She turned to Kendra. "What are you doing?" she demanded.

Kendra knew they shouldn't spill the story to him. *But oh, I so want him to like me,* she thought.

Johnny's big brown eyes widened. "Your secret's safe with me. I promise."

"Please, Audrey. What can it hurt now?" Kendra implored. Without waiting for an answer, she launched into the whole story.

Audrey stared daggers at her.

Johnny shook his head in disbelief, especially when she got to the part about hiding in Grimsby's closet. "You're puttin' me on, right?"

"No, it's all true and you can't tell a soul! Swear it," Kendra demanded.

"I promise." He held his hand over his heart in a mock pledge. "If I did tell someone, they wouldn't believe me anyway," he added. "This is so bad ass!"

Chapter 27

The clatter of coffee cups and silverware thrown unceremoniously into the dishwasher signaled the end of the afternoon rush at the small café situated in the southeast corner of Finchville's bus depot. Teresa Morgan rubbed the ache in the small of her back, thinking how glad she was to be at the ninth hour of her ten-hour shift. *I'm getting too old to be on my feet all day, serving customers who eat big and tip small,* she thought. She grabbed her coat and called out to a big, graying man at the front counter, "Ted, I'm going out back for a quick break."

"Oh yeah, you missed your afternoon break in the last rush. Go ahead, I got it covered," Ted replied. His rotund middle rested on the counter as he leaned forward, making wide circles with his bar cloth.

In the alley behind the café Teresa took some deep breaths. She could almost see some of the physical tension leave her body as she exhaled. Settling on an upturned crate, she considered how lucky she was to have a boss like Ted. No hassles — he just worked right alongside her. If he wanted her to do something he didn't command, but asked in a nice way. He and the others who worked here made this low-pay, backbreaking job bearable.

Teresa smiled to herself as she pictured Grace Magnuson, the other waitress who had befriended her from the first day she started. And Brent Grimsby, the security guard who spent as much time in the café as in the bus depot. She didn't know them well, but she hoped she could finally stay in one place long enough to have what had been impossible since she married Dan: some lasting friendships.

Teresa relaxed even more and allowed her mind to drift to her favorite daydream. *If Dan really stays on track this time, I could work part-time. It would be nice to stay home and sew curtains and be a mom. And Kendra and Toni deserve a dad who cares, too. They've put up with so much garbage from him....*

A slurred voice interrupted her happy thoughts.

"Heya baby. How's it goin'?"

Her daydream shattered at the sound of the voice. She didn't have to look to know who it was. She rose from the crate to face a very drunk ex-husband.

"Sorry to bother you at work, honey, but I wanted to tell you before you heard it from someone else." He ducked his head sheepishly, weaving from side to side.

"What?" She stiffened in anticipation of news that could only be bad.

"Boss fired me today. Said I didn't make my quotas. Course it's lies — all lies." He held his hands out to her.

Oh no! He's done it again, she thought, as she felt hot tears welling beneath her eyelids. Then rage coursed through her.

"You dirt bag!" she cried. "You don't know the difference between the truth and a lie! You just can't keep it together, can you?" Her face was bright with anger.

"T-T-Teresa, come on honey. I just had a couple of teensy-weensy ones." He lurched toward her with outstretched arms.

She pushed him away as hard as she could. She wanted him gone now and forever. *How could he show up here at work and humiliate me this way?*

Dan reeled into the brick wall of the café, and then slid slowly down into a heap of snow.

"You spineless scum! I hate you!" she screamed. "And I hate myself for letting you make a fool of me again!"

Dan hauled himself up and slapped her so hard that her glasses flew to the ground.

The screen door to the café slammed. "Folks inside say there's a problem out here. What's the trouble, Teresa?" Brent grabbed Dan and pinned him against the dumpster. "This guy bothering you?"

Teresa, too overcome to speak, sagged onto the crate again. *I've been such a dope,* she thought.

"Get your hands off me," Dan sputtered, spinning free from Brent's grip. He stared sullenly at the intruder, clenching and unclenching his fists.

"Hey, you're Teresa's ex aren't you? Well, it looks to me like she doesn't enjoy your company, so take off!" Brent's hand went to the Maglite belted at his side.

In an instant, Dan's sullenness morphed to fury. He lunged at the man, fists flying. If he had been sober, his opponent would have been out cold. As a young man, he had been a formidable boxer. But the alcohol rendered his approach too fast and his punches off the mark.

Brent only grinned in response as he deflected Dan's blows with his forearms. He pulled his Maglite from his belt. "You're asking for a flashlight shampoo, buddy! Walk away now!"

Dan glared at him, then at Teresa. Muttering obscenities, he steadied himself and staggered down the alley, his footsteps leaving a crooked trail in the snow.

"I'm sorry, Teresa," Brent handed her glasses to her. "Why don't you go on home? Just tell Ted you got sick."

She sighed heavily. "Thanks, I think I will. I do feel a little nauseous." *I can't believe how great Brent is being; having someone protect me is a whole new deal,* she thought. *Oh sure, the cops have come to my rescue, but that's their job.*

Teresa stood to go, but her knees buckled under her.

He caught her and settled her back on the crate. "Stay put while I ask Ted if I can borrow his Buick to take you home. No city bus today." He hurried into the café where he found Ted filling salt shakers.

"Sure, I can handle things here," Ted said when he heard what had happened. He rushed out to help Teresa into the car, reaching across her to hand Brent the keys. "It pulls to the right a bit. Other than that, you won't have a problem." He closed the passenger door and gave Teresa a wave.

As they drove away, Teresa leaned against the passenger window and shut her eyes to think. *Got to get myself together. There's so much to do; a new restraining order will take the rest of the afternoon. Tomorrow I'll go to the library computer and look for jobs in other towns.* She knew the routine and dreaded it, but not nearly as much as she dreaded telling Kendra she'd screwed up their lives again.

Brent's voice brought her back to the present. "Pretty quiet over there. What's going on in that busy head of yours?"

Teresa straightened and looked at her protector for the first time since she'd gotten in the car. "Just all the stuff I've got to do, like get a new order of protection. How late is the courthouse open?"

"Six o'clock, I think. But you look exhausted. How're you going to manage all the paperwork crap?" He sounded concerned. "Best to wait a day."

"No, please just take me to the daycare to pick up Toni and then to the courthouse. I know Dan. As soon as he sobers up some, he'll bust down my door in a real rage. You didn't see nothin' just now." Her eyes filled with tears. "I've had more than one late night trip to the emergency room after his visits."

They drove awhile without speaking, Brent tapping his foot and glancing sideways at Teresa. When he braked for a stoplight, he turned to her. "Look, I've got an idea. You write a note for me to pick up Toni at daycare. I'll drop you at the courthouse, and then I'll scoop up Toni and bring her to my place. Kendra can pick her up when she gets home." His voice was low and encouraging. "Toni likes me, right? I've got TV and cookies — what else do we need? She'll have a ball."

Normally, Teresa only left Toni with Kendra, but she told herself that this time is different. *He's right; I don't have the strength to take Toni with me and I've got to do something right away. Dan's getting more and more brutal in his attacks. He might even turn on Kendra, especially if she lips off to him. Her attitude toward him has been horrible lately*. She sighed wearily, "All right. But how can we let Kendra know?"

"We'll just swing by your place and you can leave her a note with my address. You just tell ol' Brent how to get there and it's done!"

Something about the way his long hands caressed the leather steering wheel made Teresa shiver inside. Her eyes flew to the patch on his uniform, and she told herself she was being paranoid. *All men aren't jerks, just because I happened to marry one. Toni will be fine with him for a couple of hours.*

Chapter 28

Kendra's hand shook as the impact of Mom's scrawled note seared through her brain.

"Your dad's at it again — showed up drunk at the café and made a scene. Brent's watching Toni 'til you get home so I can go to the courthouse. Go to 4220 Graham Ave., Unit 8, the Hearthstone Apartments next to the Laundromat we use."

Toni with that monster — by herself — oh my God! Leaning against the edge of the kitchen table, she struggled to hear her thoughts over the pounding of her heart. Turning toward the door, she realized she should call someone first. *If I call the police will they go to his place right away, or will they doubt my word because I'm "just a kid?" Toni needs help now!*

The phone rang forever before Audrey's family recording clicked on. "You've reached the Worth residence; please leave a message at the beep."

"A-A-Audrey," she stammered, "Grimsby has Toni at his apartment! I'm leaving now to get her. I-I-I'm so scared, but I don't know what else to do. It's 5:00 now. Please call the cops! And if you've got Johnny's number, call him, too!" Frantically, she punched in Mr. Campbell's number. No answer! Slamming the phone down, she raced from the empty apartment.

Chapter 28

Kendra ran as fast as she could through the growing darkness. *What did I do for this to happen to Toni?* she thought. Her feet felt like they had weights tied to them. The mounds of snow in places didn't help, and even worse — the patches of ice. Once her feet flew from beneath her but she barely noticed as she jumped up and rushed on, not bothering to brush herself off.

With no clue as to what she would do when she got there, all she could think about was how terribly long it was taking. *How could Mom put Toni and me in danger like this?* Her side began to ache and she was forced to slow to a jog. She tried to recall the tips Peg shared with her about long-distance runs, but her only thought was for Toni. *Just a few more blocks. Please don't let him hurt her!* In her mind, her sister cried out in pain and something bitter rose up in her throat. As she neared the apartments, she could see light filtering through the closed blinds of Grimsby's unit.

Summoning the courage she called up when Dad was in one of his drunken rages, she leapt up the steps and pounded on the door.

"Kendra honey, you look winded. Come on in." He held the door wide. His voice sounded relaxed, but the set of his jaw revealed something more sinister. "Just fixin' a little supper. You and Toni might as well stay. I don't think your mom's gonna feel like cooking. She's havin' a real bad day."

A little voice came from another room, "Kendra, come here."

Kendra rushed toward the sound of the voice to find Toni happily playing with a doll house on the living room floor. Relief nearly overcame Kendra as she realized her sister seemed fine.

"Can we stay? Look at this, Kenra," Toni said rearranging a miniature crib and rocking chair in a pretend nursery. "Brent bought it just for me." A Powerpuff cartoon flickered on the television screen.

Kendra bent to catch her breath so she could say, "No, we've got to get home," but when she straightened, she saw Grimsby throw the deadbolt on the door and fold his arms over his chest. *We're trapped.* A visual of the young girls in the photos she and Audrey had discovered in the closet floated eerily before her eyes. *Would she and Toni soon be like those sad creatures? Or worse?*

"I guess we could stay," she mumbled as her jellied knees gave way and she sank onto the rug beside Toni.

"Great — I think it's ready," he said." Just a sec and I'll serve it up." He gestured to a small table with straight-back chairs between the kitchenette and the living room. Showing a toothy grin, he began heaping mounds of something resembling regurgitated dog food onto plates.

Kendra weakly lifted Toni from her play and took her by the hand to the table.

Grimsby delivered the three plates with a flourish.

Kendra stared at the Hamburger Helper on her plate and wondered how she could eat even one mouthful.

Toni picked up her fork and dove into her meal. "I wanna play with the doll house some more. Soon as I'm done eating. 'Okay?"

Their captor laughed. Then his eyes slid to Kendra, who sat stiffly beside Toni. "Dig in, young lady. You've got to keep your energy up for the evening ahead." He smiled the same black, oily smile he'd had the day he'd made a pass at her.

I can't believe I was so naïve then, believing he would help me find Cloud's murderer. Goosebumps crept up her arms, neck and scalp. She searched her mind for a way to escape. Glancing around, she wished with all her heart for some miracle to save them, but all she saw was a messy apartment.

Grimsby jumped up. "Forgot the drinks."

As he rummaged in the refrigerator, Kendra suddenly knew what she had to do. She took a deep breath to steady herself and whispered in Toni's ear to run for help at her signal.

"Why?" Toni whispered back, her blue eyes wide with wonder.

"Because Brent's a really bad man," Kendra replied. *Got to stay calm so Toni doesn't freak,* she thought.

"You mean he's the Boogie Man?" Her forehead wrinkled in concentration.

"Yes. When I open the door, you run as fast as you can to the Laundromat – it's straight out the door! Tell them to call the police." She patted Toni's leg reassuringly. As Grimsby returned with two glasses of milk, she lowered her head over her plate.

"Now for my beer," he said, turning back to the kitchenette. "What are you two whispering about? You wouldn't be keeping secrets from ol' Brent, would you?"

He knows what we're up to but he doesn't think we can get away. As their captor turned toward the kitchenette, she jumped from her chair and dove as hard as she could at the back of his legs like she'd seen football players do. He went down hard, grazing his temple on the counter's edge.

Kendra jumped up as he lay there stunned. She flew to the door, threw the deadbolt, and flung the door open. "Come on Toni, run! Run as fast as you can!"

Toni sprang for the door, her blonde curls flying behind her.

Kendra's chest stung from the impact with Grimsby's legs, but she was overjoyed at the sight of her sister running through the darkness toward the glowing sign of the Laundromat. As she turned to go in the opposite direction, she felt her feet leave the floor and her body being slammed into the wall. He yanked her to her feet and a wrenching pain shot up her arm. She looked up at her captor who held her to him in an iron grip. A trickle of blood oozed down the side of his face.

"Oh no you don't!" He gaped out the door, but Toni was already out of sight. "You just had to complicate things, didn't you?" He spun Kendra towards him and backhanded her so hard her neck made a popping noise. "Where did you tell her to go?"

"To the neighbors. It's too late," she cried. "They're already calling the police." She knew he wouldn't believe her bluff, but she had to try.

He slammed the door shut and pulled her toward the bedroom.

Chapter 29

"Okay you little bitch, you asked for it. Come on. You and me are going for a ride." Grimsby's face was pinched and ugly. He yanked Kendra by the arm and moved her through the apartment. He pulled handcuffs from his dresser and cuffed her to the bed frame.

Her cheek still stung from the slap and her neck had a dull ache. Hot tears burned her eyelids. She wanted to tell him how she hated him and what a monster he was, but she could only watch as he stuffed clothes and money into an overnight bag.

Retrieving a gun from its hiding place, he stuck it in his belt. He threw on his coat, then unlocked the cuffs and thrust her coat at her.

As she struggled to put it on, Kendra realized she couldn't move her arm.

"Put the damned coat on," he growled.

Pain shot from her fingertips to her shoulder, but she managed to slide into the sleeve.

Grimsby grabbed Ted's car keys and propelled them toward the front door. "Now in case anyone sees us, you're going to act like everything's fine and I'm just taking you home. Right?" He pulled her close and squeezed her injured arm.

Kendra felt the nose of the pistol pressed into her side. Fighting back the blackness that threatened to envelop her, she nodded a yes.

"Good, 'cuz I want it to be just you and me on our big adventure, darlin'."

Kendra steeled herself for the walk to the car. Later she could fall apart, but right now she had to buy Toni time. She choked back the tears and lifted her chin.

Grimsby's strong, bony hand pulled her past the cooling food and Toni's coat on a low stool. He flung the door open and stepped back for Kendra to go first. They walked the short distance to Ted's car; she watched numbly as he unlocked the passenger door and motioned for her to get in.

He snapped a cuff on her left wrist as she sat down and locked her to the gearshift column. Getting behind the wheel, he stowed the gun in the door pocket. He threw the bag in the back seat and started the engine. As he wheeled the sedan from the parking lot, Kendra heard the squeal of the tires on the pavement.

They headed in the opposite direction from her home and an overwhelming despair washed over her. She sank down into the seat and closed her eyes. She was vaguely aware of Grimsby talking to himself about how driving Ted's car instead of his would give him an advantage.

"They'll be on the lookout for my old beater instead." He chuckled.

After awhile, she remembered seeing a news story about a boy who'd been taken. He'd paid attention to his surroundings and when he managed to escape, he was able to help the cops find his abductor. *If I somehow survive this nightmare, even the smallest bit of information could help,* she thought.

She leaned as far away from Grimsby as the handcuffs would allow and watched the route they drove. She noted the time on the dashboard clock at 6:10 p.m. They were heading north toward Interstate 80. The Piggly Wiggly, Taco Bell and Kentucky Fried Chicken flew by, then Finchville's two sprawling car lots on the outskirts of town. Soon the dim outlines of occasional farmhouses and the cornfields where the sandhill cranes would stop to feed on their spring migration were all she could make out. The realization that she might never see the huge birds again pierced her heart.

They drove in silence for what seemed like forever. Kendra cradled her aching arm to her body and fought to be brave. They were miles from Finchville, but they hadn't reached the interstate yet. *I hope Toni's okay,* she thought.

"You know, you made a pile of trouble for me today but I think I'm gonna forgive you. You know why?" He glanced her way.

She stared out the passenger window, saying nothing. The energy she needed to answer him was as nonexistent as the cranes.

"Speak up, little bitch! You know why?"

She felt a heavy hand on her shoulder. Kendra mumbled a "no," and hunched further down in her seat.

"Because you're going to be a lot more fun than the others. They were easy bait, but you're a fighter. I like that. You were scared as hell but even then, you hung in there. Fallin' apart at the supper table, yet you jumped me. Makes my juices flow to think about it."

Kendra wouldn't look his way, but knew he was smiling into the night. "You murdered my friend, didn't you?" She couldn't believe her own daring.

"You think?" He swallowed happily. "And those dumb cops have no clue. We've got plenty of time to get away. By the time they figure out what your little brat sister's saying, we'll be in Colorado."

Kendra watched his big hand reach over and squeeze her thigh hard. She bit her lip, refusing to give him the satisfaction of knowing he'd hurt her. The lights of the interstate came into view and the big car barreled onto the on-ramp and headed west. Now the darkened landscape fell away at a maddening pace. She glanced at the speedometer — 90 miles an hour. "Isn't the speed limit 70?"

"I know what you're up to. You think those small town cops will catch us if we're going slower, but it ain't gonna happen, darlin'. They're probably still trying to find their badges." He laughed, but then seemed to be thinking. "Guys do get stopped for stupid stuff though." The passing landscape slowed and he pulled a pack of Marlboros from his shirt pocket and lit one up. "Settle in, sweetheart. Might be a long night." He shifted in his seat. "Why don't you see what's on the radio?" When there was no response, he let the cigarette hang loosely from his lips and punched the buttons until the sound of a twangy song filled the car. "How's that? Good, huh?"

Kendra hated country music, but something told her to agree. She nodded her head and watched the off-ramp for the town of Kearney slide by and knew the little town of Lexington would be next. In a strange way, all those moves running from Dad were helping her keep track of where she was. North Platte would be another 100 miles and then the Colorado border would be close. She wasn't sure what that would mean. *Would the Nebraska cops have to stop at the border?* Probably, but she was sure the Colorado police would take up the chase. It scared her to think she was getting further and further from home. *Oh, if only they could catch us before the state line*! Again, she thought about Toni. She pictured her sister running into the night toward the Laundromat. *She's so little. What if a car didn't see her in the parking lot?* She pushed the scary scene from her mind and reminded herself to pay attention to where they were.

As the miles flew by, she kept her terror at bay by thinking of ways to get away from this madman. He had to stop sometime. As they approached North Platte, she said, "I need to use the bathroom." Her heart sank as they flew past exits advertising gas and food. "Please," she whined. "I'm going to wet myself."

He looked at her skeptically and kept driving long past North Platte and through the vastness of the prairie landscape. Finally, the car slowed and pulled off the freeway onto the gravel embankment. "Let's go," he said as he unlocked the handcuff and led her a few yards away from the car.

Please let someone see us, she thought. "I can't go with you watching," she begged.

"Better get used to it. I'm going to be seeing a lot more than this," he growled. "Here, I'll show you how it's done." He unzipped his pants and began relieving himself.

The sound of his urine hitting the gravel made Kendra's stomach lurch. *But I've got to play along,* she thought. So she pulled her jeans and panties down and squatted. At first she didn't think she could go, but she hadn't lied when she'd told him she would wet herself. Eventually her bladder released.

He laughed. "See. We're gonna do lots of fun stuff together." Then he yanked her up and hugged her to him.

"Stop!" Kendra tried to pull her clothes up, but he gripped her good arm and her right arm was useless.

He reached down and helped her straighten her clothes. Then before she could react, he cupped his large hand around her chin and kissed her hard. Panic made her knees buckle and he dragged her toward the car. She wanted to spit out the vile taste of tobacco, but instead fought back the sobs rising in her throat.

"Whatsa matter darlin'? Feelin' a little weak? Let me help." He lifted her easily into his arms and headed back to the Buick.

As he closed the handcuff around her wrist, she realized she was living her nightmare — this evil monster was going to torture and kill her. She thought about Cloud and knew the horror her friend must have felt when she was kidnapped.

The next three hours seemed like thirty. They were over the Colorado border now and the next big town was Sterling. According to the dashboard clock, they'd be there about midnight. Sterling came and went and he drove on, the rhythmic bumps in the surface of the freeway lulling Kendra. If she hadn't been a prisoner, she would've been fast asleep long ago. More time passed and Kendra lost track of where they were. Suddenly she felt the car swerve and saw his head snap up. *He's getting sleepy!*

He opened his window and the cold air rushed in as he pulled another cigarette from his pocket. "Talk to me, darlin'. How old are you anyway?"

Kendra stared silently out the passenger window.

"Come on! Don't wanna die in a fiery crash, do you? Gotta keep me awake!" When she still didn't speak, he reached across and smacked her. Then he grabbed her jacket and shook her hard. As Kendra tried to curl into a ball, he chuckled. "Well, that woke me up."

After a while, he announced, "Rest stop comin' up. We'll get a few minutes shut eye." Tall light standards soon loomed into view and he pulled the Buick into a large parking area. With the exception of two semi-trucks, they were the only ones there. He pushed his seat back, stretched his long legs and leaned back. "Close your eyes, darlin'."

Kendra was exhausted but she didn't think she could sleep. Fearing more violence, she turned her face toward him so he could see her eyelids flutter shut. Soon she heard a gentle snoring and looked to see his head slumped to one side. *I've got to think of a way out of this,* she thought, but her muddled brain refused to work.

*****

She startled awake to the sound of the driver's car seat sliding forward. "Takin' a leak." He was out of the car before she could respond. When he returned, she told him she had to go, too.

"Figures," he grumbled. He unlocked the cuff and took her by the arm to the entrance of a low grey building. "I'm gonna stand right here." He fished a cigarette from his shirt pocket. "If anybody shows up, you're my daughter. Got that?"

She nodded and walked on shaky legs into the restroom. As soon as she exited the stall, she looked around for something to write on. Grabbing a piece of toilet paper and a pink lip gloss from her jacket pocket, she wrote: *Help! Kendra Morgan. Finchville, Nebraska.* The paper tore as Grimsby called out, "Get your butt out here or I'm comin' in!" With a sinking feeling that the note wasn't readable, she abandoned it on the counter between the sinks. As she stumbled down the sidewalk, she looked east toward home and saw the morning light gathering on the horizon.

They drove on in a southerly direction. Soon the sun was fully up and Kendra saw they were on I-25. Her stomach growled.

"Hungry, huh? I could use some chow, too." At the next exit, he pulled off and into the closest fast food place with a drive through. "What's your pleasure?" he asked as they waited behind a red pickup.

She wanted to ignore him but then thought better of it. *In case I get a chance to escape, I need to keep my strength up.* "Breakfast sandwich," she muttered.

"Please?" he grinned through stained teeth.

"Please," she mumbled reluctantly.

"See. It's not hard to make nice with 'ol Brent. Might even get you some tater tots."

He ordered their food, then pulled his coat from the back seat and threw it over the gearshift column to hide the handcuff. He pulled forward to the pickup window. "Wouldn't want anybody to get the wrong idea," he said. "Keep that hand under the coat. Hear me?"

"That's $9.67, sir," a teen girl with a bad case of acne said. As she bent forward to take the money, Kendra tried to catch her eye. The girl glanced at her and as she leaned forward to hand the bags out the window, she looked again — more intently this time. Kendra mouthed the words "help me" as they pulled away, hardly daring to hope that the girl understood.

They continued traveling south, with Grimsby wolfing down his breakfast as he drove. Kendra held her injured arm next to her body and did her best to eat her sandwich. The terrain grew steeper. She watched what she thought was a forest of Ponderosa Pines whiz past. A flock of red-winged blackbirds sprang up from the underbrush. This was unfamiliar terrain, but the beauty of the clear blue sky and snow-covered countryside made her heart ache. *The world doesn't care about my suffering,* she thought. *If only I could fly away like those birds.*

"They'll think I headed through Kansas," Grimsby said to himself. He turned to Kendra. "There's a little out-of-the-way place we can hole up near Albuquerque. We'll have us some real fun there." He smiled. "Be there soon, darlin'." He reached over to squeeze her thigh again, but suddenly something had his attention in the rearview mirror. Kendra looked out her side mirror. Flashing red and blue lights!

Chapter 30

Grimsby jammed the accelerator to the floor, slamming Kendra's head into the headrest. "They can't catch us – this baby can flat out move!"

As the big car leaped forward, sirens wailed. Kendra's ears had never heard a more welcome sound.

He began passing cars ahead of them so fast that she was terrified to look at the speedometer. She closed her eyes and held her breath. The miles fell away and she wondered how long before the car failed to make one of the mountainous curves.

Suddenly she realized the sound of the sirens had stopped. *He can't be outrunning them!* She opened her eyes to look over her shoulder and counted three police cars still in pursuit. *Thank goodness!*

"Dammit!" He yelled.

Kendra turned back to see a heavy barricade come into view. She stared at Grimsby in horror. *Would he stop?* With each passing second, the barrier and uniformed figures standing by their vehicles grew larger. She turned to implore him to stop, but the words stuck in her throat.

The veins at his temple throbbed. "Frickin' assholes!" he yelled.

Kendra closed her eyes again and braced for the impact. Instead her head snapped to the side as she heard the squeal of tires. The car skidded to a sideways stop against the blockade. The smell of burning rubber filling her nose was such a relief! She was still alive!

She could see an army of cops and vehicles stationed behind the blockade. *He's going to hold me hostage,* she thought. The next few minutes were a blur. Kendra wanted to jump from the car and run — somewhere...anywhere. She yanked at the handcuff holding her fast to the gearshift column. Without the key, she could only watch the scene unfold before her.

A voice boomed out, "Get out of the car! Put your hands on your head!"

At first, Grimsby raised his hands in the air as if surrendering.

"That's good," the megaphone voice continued. "Now come on out! Slowly!"

He nodded and opened the car door but in the same instant, he reached into the door pocket to grab his gun. Using the door as a shield, he pointed the weapon toward the barricade. "I'll give you the girl if you let me go!"

A laugh boomed out into the stillness. "You can't be serious! Do you see how many people we got here? SWAT included? Take a look around, man!"

Grimsby turned his head and for the first time realized he was surrounded. With painstaking slowness, he looked for an escape route.

"You best hurry! These SWAT guys love target practice!" The voice continued.

He lowered the gun. It hung from his arm like an anchor holding him there.

Once again, the order was crisply delivered: "That's it! Drop the weapon! Place your hands over your head!"

Suddenly Kendra heard the crunch of gravel flying beneath her kidnapper's boots as he sprinted down the shoulder of the interstate and into a field.

"Get him!", someone shouted and a mob of deputies raced away, but Grimsby's long legs were gaining ground.

Kendra couldn't believe what she was seeing. *He's escaping!* she thought. As she watched, two officers jumped into a nearby patrol car and squealed away. The cruiser left the road and bounced through the field, mowing down frozen corn stalks in its path. He stumbled over the hard earth, but he was out of breath and out of time. The driver arced around to cut him off and bounded out of the vehicle as it swayed on its axis.

She saw the officer throw himself with incredible speed at Grimsby, wrestle him to the ground, and pin his arms behind him. He cuffed him and pulled him to his knees, then to his feet. Another officer snatched something from the ground. *Probably the gun,* she thought. Seeing him on his knees in that instant triggered an indescribable feeling in Kendra. *It's finally over! He can't terrorize me anymore.*

Uniforms ran in from every direction. She watched as his hunched frame stumbled away between two officers who gripped him like a vise. Hot tears scorched her cheeks.

A young policewoman approached, opened the passenger door, and gently touched Kendra's shoulder. "Everything's okay now," she said. Seeing the handcuffs, she pulled a key from her pants pocket and leaned across Kendra to free her. "These look like standard issue cuffs. My key should work just fine."

Kendra's tears turned to sobs.

The officer put her arm around Kendra to steady her, and helped her from the car. "We'll take you to the hospital, just to get checked out. Normal procedure – not to worry," she said softly as she handed her young charge a tissue and slowly walked her toward a nearby police car. "We'll call your mom right away."

"Is my little sister okay?" Kendra sputtered.

"Yes, she's just fine," the woman replied. "What about you? You're holding your arm kind of funny."

The kindness in her eyes made Kendra feel a little better. "I think it might be broken," she said, her sobs subsiding to shudders. "But I'll be all right." Blowing her nose hard, she took a deep breath and settled against the back seat. She heard the trunk open and close and the officer handed her a wool blanket. Pulling it tight under her chin, she suddenly couldn't wait to see her mom. The anger and frustration that she'd felt whenever she thought of Mom in recent months were replaced with a longing to be held and comforted.

*****

The doors of the Denver Children's Hospital opened wide and Kendra's mom ran to the patrol car with an orderly pushing a wheelchair behind her. She slid into the back seat next to Kendra and hugged her. "Are you all right? My God, I couldn't believe it when I heard Brent had taken you! Can you ever forgive me?" Teresa scrubbed her forehead.

Kendra couldn't believe her eyes. "How did you get here so fast?" she asked as she curled into Teresa's arms.

"Someone found your note at a rest area. Then the Colorado cops said they were pretty sure you'd been spotted at a fast food place."

That girl at the drive through! She actually did something! And someone at the rest stop, too! They'll always be my angels! Kendra thought.

Teresa brushed her daughter's hair back from her forehead. Are you sure you're okay?"

"My arm hurts. But go on, you were telling me how you got here."

"Oh, yeah. Sorry. I'm just so glad to see you! Well, when Detective Goodwin heard the Colorado force was closing in on your location, she put a police patrol helicopter from Omaha on standby. And when she got the news that they had their suspect in custody and you were safe, she said I could fly along with her."

"Oh Mom, I was a dope thinking Audrey and I could get Cloud's murderer on our own. I should've told you, especially when we were pretty sure it was Grimsby! But I didn't think you'd believe me after I wrongly accused Billy Ray." She looked into her mother's worried face.

"You know, I might not have. I'm ashamed to admit it, but I might not have. I won't doubt you ever again, not after all that's happened. I'll make it up to you…" Teresa's voice cracked.

"Excuse me ma'am, but we need to get your daughter inside," the orderly's voice interrupted them.

Teresa brushed the tears from her eyes. "Come on, Kendra. We'll talk more after the doctor looks at you. Oh, and Toni's fine. She's been bragging to everyone about how you 'made the bad man go boomie.'" A hint of a smile crossed her face as she helped Kendra out of the car and into the wheelchair.

Kendra objected, "I'm okay, Mom." But she was secretly glad. Her legs felt like mush. And her arm throbbed like crazy.

In the emergency room, the doctor examined her and determined that with the exception of some bad bruises and a fractured arm, she was fine. "I think we can set the limb pretty quickly and get you back to Nebraska," he pronounced. "I'd like you to spend the night in the hospital there though. You're going to have some discomfort with that wing."

It wasn't long before Kendra, sporting a neon green cast, found herself being wheeled to an ambulance for the trip to Finchville. "We can't afford this!" she exclaimed as her mom climbed in beside her.

"Detective Goodwin said not to worry about it," Teresa said. "She'll want to talk to you later, but you just relax now. The doctor gave you something to help you sleep."

Whatever medication the doctor had given her, it must've been super-good because Kendra fell into a deep sleep and only roused herself when they arrived at Finchville's small hospital. The staff whisked her through the door and into a room while Mom stayed behind to fill out the paperwork. A grandmotherly nurse helped her into bed — she was discovering how hard it was to do things with one arm. The nurse bustled away and returned a few minutes later with red Jell-O and a packet of graham crackers. Halfway through the Jell-O cup, the spoon grew heavy. She was vaguely aware of the feel of cool sheets as she was being tucked in.

Chapter 31

The next afternoon Kendra woke to see Audrey at the foot of her hospital bed. Her friend gripped the bed rail so hard her knuckles were white. A sudden remembrance of what had happened flooded Kendra's mind like the bright winter light that filled the room.

"Where's Mom?" Kendra asked.

"When I got here, she said she'd go see about finding you something to eat. You missed breakfast and lunch," Audrey said. "Toni was bouncing around the room like a beach ball, waiting for you to wake up. She left you a calling card." She pointed at Kendra's cast.

A lopsided pink valentine bloomed on the fluorescent green cast and brought a smile to Kendra's lips. "Can't wait to give the little squirt a major hug," she said.

"How are you anyway? You look terrible!" Audrey said.

"Gee, thanks," Kendra answered sarcastically. "I think I'm fine. I just needed some extra z's." She gingerly touched her cheek.

"It's all black and blue. What happened?" Audrey settled herself on a chair next to Kendra.

"The slime ball slapped me when Toni got away. It's sore, but hey, it could've been so much worse."

"So, tell me all about it," Audrey demanded.

"Okay, but I need to wake up a little more." Her head felt like she was in a deep fog. Then she remembered the heavy-duty drug. She motioned for Audrey to hand her the glass of water at her bedside, and said, "You go first. I can't wait to hear what happened with you guys."

"All right, but then it's your turn." Audrey drew a breath. "When I got home from soccer practice and heard your message, I could hardly understand it; you sounded so hysterical! I called Mr. Campbell and he said he'd be right over. While I was waiting, I called your mom and told her we were coming to pick her up. I knew she'd lose it if I told her the truth, so I said I'd explain when we got there. Then I hung up real quick before she could ask any questions." Audrey laughed. "I had no idea Mr. Campbell could move so fast. He was at my door in a flash."

"So what did you tell my mom when you picked her up?" Kendra asked.

"I sat in the back, looked at my iPhone, and prayed she wouldn't ask me anything. Mr. Campbell was so cool. I wish you could've seen him. He did everything right — drove fast and talked slow. He made up a story about how you had called and wanted us to pick you and Toni up because Ted's car wouldn't start."

"When we got close to Grimsby's apartment, we saw tons of cop cars at the Laundromat. They had Toni sitting in one of them. She'd already told them about the 'Boogie Man,' but they didn't know where she'd come from. Little kids don't make much sense, even at the best of times."

"Tell me about it," Kendra said.

"I filled them in on how you and I suspected Grimsby of being Cloud's killer. That was when your mom lost it. She actually collapsed. But Detective Goodwin was there and told her they really needed her help to get you back. Your mom snapped right out of it and gave a description of Ted's Buick."

Audrey stopped to catch her breath. "Then they took us to the police station to wait. It was hours and hours before the Colorado cops radioed that they had Grimsby in custody close to the New Mexico border. When they said you were all right, your mom started to perk up."

"Poor Mom." Kendra shook her head.

"No kidding! Now you tell me your story," Audrey said.

"Okay." She stretched her good arm overhead, checking for any stiffness. "Hey, I feel pretty good, considering."

As she spoke, Johnny Haskins stuck his head in the door. "Mind if I come in?" He clutched a single red rose.

Audrey's eyes widened at the sight of Johnny. She whispered quickly in Kendra's ear. "Johnny 'borrowed' his dad's old tractor to get to the police station when none of his family was home to drive him into town. He definitely likes you!"

Kendra waved him in as she tried to hide her reaction to Audrey's words. *Johnny took a real chance driving without a license, even if it was on a John Deere,* she thought. Then she remembered the horrible hospital gown she was wearing. *My hair must look like an orangutan on steroids.* She burrowed beneath the covers.

"You're just in time; Kendra's going to tell her side of the story," Audrey said.

Running her fingers through her matted hair, Kendra launched into her version of events.

When she finished, Audrey said, "You were so brave! I could've never tackled Grimsby like that! Oh, guess what? A reporter from *The Morning Sun* showed up and asked if she could interview you and me when you feel up to it!" Audrey's eyes were huge.

"Wow!" Kendra gasped.

"We're famous, I guess," Audrey replied and shook her head in disbelief.

"I just wanted to find Cloud's murderer," Kendra said.

"Turns out the scum of the earth is suspected of other murders, too. In fact, there's another girl missing from right here in Finchville! Her family didn't report her gone right away 'cuz they thought she'd run off with her boyfriend. Detective Goodwin's sure Grimsby did something to her. Remember the box of girls' things we found in his apartment?"

"How could I forget?" Kendra replied.

"The detective told me they found the girl's earmuffs there! We stopped a serial killer, Kendra! Incredible, huh?"

Kendra covered her mouth in surprise. "Yeah, I remember — the hot pink earmuffs! OMG!"

"Oh yeah, you two are gonna be the hot gossip all over town!" Johnny said. "I bet the school will even have an assembly for you."

Kendra and Audrey looked at each other and suddenly burst into spasms of giggles.

Kendra knew their reaction wasn't right, considering another girl had gone missing. But there was no denying that a truckload of tension lifted as they realized they were safe from the depraved monster that had killed their friend.

"That wasn't all that happened," Johnny said. "Peg came to the cop shop when she heard about your kidnapping. Both she and Mr. Campbell apologized over and over to your mom for keeping the investigation a secret from her. They both said they had no idea how deep into the case you were. Your mom was very cool about it. In fact, she and Peg seemed to really hit it off."

"Really?" Kendra asked. "They're so different!"

"It's true," Audrey agreed. "And guess what else?"

"There's more?" Kendra asked.

"Mr. Campbell announced that he and Laura are engaged! I think he wanted to cheer everyone up. It was pretty heavy there for awhile," Audrey said.

"Well, that certainly makes me happy!" Kendra said. She looked at Johnny and for some reason she didn't understand, her normally pale complexion turned bright red.

He chose that moment to thrust the rose at her. "Uh, here — this is for you," he mumbled. In an instant, his face was as crimson as Kendra's.

"Well, well, look at you two," Audrey said. "Do you want me to leave?" She laughed.

Kendra and Johnny shook their heads vehemently and cried "No!"

At that moment, Kendra heard hurried footsteps in the hall, and an excited voice called out, "Kenra, we got you a sammich!" Toni burst through the door with Teresa close behind. Toni clambered onto the bed and threw her arms around her sister's neck. "Did you see what I did?" She pointed at the artwork adorning Kendra's cast.

"Yeah, very cool," Kendra said as she returned Toni's hug.

"We got the bad man, didn't we?" Toni smiled a smug little grin.

"Sure did," Kendra replied.

Toni opened her mouth to say something else, but stopped when she saw Johnny. She slid off the bed and stood as close as she could to him. "I know who you are."

Johnny looked startled. "Yeah?"

"You were there when we was waiting for Kenra." She puffed her little chest out. "Are you Kenra's boyfriend?"

Johnny was speechless. He stared at his feet.

"You don't have any little sisters or brothers, do you?" Kendra asked.

Johnny could only shake his head.

"No need to freak," Kendra said. "They're just like us, only with over-size heads and short necks."

That brought a smile to Johnny's face, but Kendra could see he still felt awkward.

"Come on, Toni. Quit bothering Johnny. Help me with Kendra's lunch," Teresa interjected.

Toni grabbed the lunch sack from her mom and jumped back on the bed. Johnny saw his chance for a getaway. "Well, I gotta get going," he said.

"Me, too," Audrey chimed in. "Call me when you get home tonight."

"Okay," Kendra said as she took a huge bite of sandwich and handed the other half to Toni. As she watched her friends leave, she was overwhelmed with a sense of thankfulness for them, and her family, and the fact that she was truly safe.

Chapter 32

Several days passed before Kendra's life returned to normal, with the exception of a morbid interest in the case from the locals. Because life moved so slowly in Finchville, its citizens loved a new topic for gossip. There hadn't been this much excitement since the tornado of '95 when the Andrews' billy goat was scooped up and deposited unharmed over a mile away. Everywhere Kendra went, she was asked to tell her version of the events surrounding Cloud's death. From neighbors to complete strangers, they begged to hear it all — from the very beginning of Kendra and Audrey's investigation to the capture.

Friday night, Kendra looked up from her English paper. "Mom, people are driving me nuts."

"What?" Teresa finished shoving the leftovers in the refrigerator.

"People I don't even know are coming up to me to find out about the case. I'm sick of telling the story over and over."

"You don't have to talk to them, you know."

"I don't?"

"Just tell them you've told the police and the media what happened and you're moving on."

"Good idea. I'll do it!"

"I'd like your opinion on something, too," Teresa said.

"Oh?" Kendra asked. She watched her mom pull up a chair and settle opposite her at the table. *Something's up; Mom never asks me about anything,* she thought. *And now she wants my opinion!*

"I've decided to stick it out this time. I'm tired of running from your dad, and I know you are, too. We're staying here, no matter what." The determination in Teresa's voice was unmistakable.

This was the first time her mom had brought up Dad falling back into his old ways since all the commotion at Mom's work. Kendra had been expecting an announcement that they'd be moving again and couldn't hide her surprise. "W-w-what?" she stammered.

"I was all set to run again, but I started thinking about it. You showed me what a coward I've been when you risked so much for your friend and your sister. I owe you and Toni some courage, too." Teresa straightened in her chair.

"But Mom, you know how Dad is. It's just a matter of time before he barges in and starts knocking you around again." Kendra couldn't believe she was actually trying to talk her mom out of this. It was the one thing she had longed for: a real home with friends who would be there for more than a few months. She didn't dare think about how much she would miss Audrey, Johnny, Peg, and Mr. Campbell.

"That night while I was waiting for you at the station, Peg came in to sit with us," Teresa continued. "We started talking and I told her about your dad, the latest restraining order, and all that. She said if I get tough, he'll back down.

So that's what I plan to do, but I want you to buy into it, too." Teresa looked intently into her daughter's eyes.

"So what are you going to do?" Kendra asked, marveling at her mom's words.

"I'll start the process of getting support money from him. Of course, like before, he'll be here raising hell when he finds out. When he does, Peg wants me to call her. She knows some mean-looking guys — weightlifter types. She claims when he realizes we've got back-up, he'll quit harassing us."

"Wow!" Kendra said.

Teresa drew a deep breath. "Actually, I'm pretty scared, but Peg told me about meetings I can go to with other women who have the same problems. When I first met her and she insisted that we go to the police about Billy Ray, I didn't like her. Now I know it was because she was making me face my responsibilities."

Kendra suddenly felt so happy she thought she would explode. "Mom, I'm so proud of you! Of course I want to do this; it's time we stood up to Dad!"

Teresa reached across the table and held Kendra's hand. "I'm proud of you, too, honey. You've grown up so much. With your encouragement, I think I can do what I should've done a long time ago."

"I don't feel that grown up, Mom. I've been putting off something I promised Billy Ray that I'd do."

"What?" Teresa asked, mystified.

Searching her mom's face, she said, "I told him I'd get Cloud's shoes back for him. They're being used as evidence, but Detective Goodwin says her parents will get them back when the trial's over. But I don't want to cause them any more grief."

Teresa thought for a moment. "Go ahead and call. You may be surprised." She nudged Kendra.

Kendra rose and went to the phone. "Mrs. Nicholson?" Her voice shook.

"Yes?"

"This is Kendra Morgan. I was a friend of Cloud's."

"Of course, I know who you are. We've wanted to thank you for helping find justice for her. You don't know the relief it's brought us."

Kendra gulped. "You're welcome, Mrs. Nicholson. Look, I have a huge, huge favor to ask. If it's too out there, just say so." She hurriedly explained Billy Ray's part in the case and his wish to have Cloud's shoes to share with his critters.

There was a long silence and Kendra thought about hanging up.

"I guess it's the least we can do to show our thanks for what you and Billy Ray and everyone else did."

"Oh, thank you! He'll be so happy." She sighed and put the phone down.

Her mom smiled at her across the room.

"Oh Mom, I feel good...like the case is finally closed. At least my part in it." She sighed again, a very big sigh this time. "I can't wait to tell Billy Ray."

Chapter 33

Mushing through the dirty brown slush on the way to the park, Kendra barely noticed her bleak surroundings. Her arm throbbed a little from the cold and she thought about how nice it would be to be rid of her cast in a few weeks. The February sun filtered weakly through the trees, casting long shadows across the pathway. Her mind traveled back to that Saturday morning at the community center where she'd spotted the tip of Cloud's favorite barrette in Billy Ray's pocket. For the gazillionth time, she thanked her lucky stars that in spite of her foolishness, she'd gotten through the whole experience safely. *If I had it to do over again, would I?* she thought. *Probably.*

Then her mind traveled to the wonderful friends she'd made since then: Mr. Campbell, Billy Ray, Peg, and of course, Johnny. And she and Audrey were better friends than ever. She wasn't sure how to describe it, but she wanted Audrey to always be in her life. Finchville could finally be a place to belong. A place to call home.

"Hey!" a deep voice called quietly from a clearing.

She looked to her right to see Billy Ray tearing a loaf of French bread into small bits for a flock of sparrows. "Dirt's frozen," he said. "They can't find a thing for their little bellies."

Slowly, so she wouldn't disturb the birds, Kendra crept closer. "It shouldn't be too much longer before spring's here," she replied. "I know I'm sure ready."

"And how," he said, sounding very mature.

It made Kendra laugh. "I've got some good news for you. When the trial's over, Mrs. Nicholson told me she expects to get Cloud's things back. She wants to give you the shoes and the hair clip as a way to thank you for your help."

Billy Ray's eyebrows went up. His round face grew rounder as a smile stole from ear to ear. "Really? I'm her hero?"

"Absolutely — just like Batman!" Kendra felt warm inside in spite of the 40-degree temperature.

"My critters will be so happy. The shine and the sparkles…I wish you could see them play." He stopped picking at the bread as he concentrated on what he wanted to say next. "Know what?"

"What?" Kendra asked.

"If the squirrels get to 'em before the crows, the crows will watch where they hide 'em and dig 'em up later." It was Billy Ray's turn to laugh.

"I'll see them play. Don't you worry. I'm going to be here for a very, very long time." She reached out and touched his shoulder and smiled a smile every bit as big as his. Then she stood on tiptoe and put her good arm up to hug him. Billy Ray bent and folded her into his bulk, the melting snow running in fast rivulets beneath their boots.

CPSIA information can be obtained at www.ICGtesting.com
Printed in the USA
BVOW03s1529281014

372668BV00007B/9/P